# Train of Thoughts

By

## Creative Writing Students of
## La Quinta High School

La Quinta High School
Westminster, California

# Train of Thoughts

**Edited and Compiled by:** Amanda LaPera
**Senior Copy Editors:** Jennifer Chau, Monica Van
**Copy Editors:** Derek Nguyen, Kimberly Nguyen
**Section Editors:** Kristy Diep, Tuyet Duong, Christine Ha, Jayson Mitchell, Jenny Nguyen, Vincent Nguyen, Thong Pham, Alex Quang, Mikayla Reilly
**Design Editors:** Becky Lee, Maggie Tieu
**Cover Designed by:** Becky Lee
**Interior Editors:** Kenna B. James, Kristy Nguyen

Published by La Quinta High School Creative Writing Class

Dedicated to those lost in their own thoughts and seeking their way out

# Table of Contents

# OPEN A BOOK

## By Kimberly Nguyen

Open a book,
Pull out a pencil
Make the world yours,
And don't use a stencil
For the world is what you make it,
And there's no time to fake it

If you want to go far
Just be who you are
Because it'd be a shame
If we all were the same

So pull out that pencil,
Throw away that stencil,
Open that book
And give it a look
For an author's true self
Lives on the bookshelf

# FREEDOM FOR A DAY

## By Derek Nguyen

BROWN, CRINKLED LEAVES FLEW through the air, spiraling into the overcast sky. Through a window in the clouds golden light seeped through, bathing the clearing in warmth. A pair of mottled quails bobbed their heads through the waving grass, pecking at the soil. A branch snapped, and they vanished with heavy flaps and falling feathers. Walking out from the fringes of the trees, a soldier shielded his eyes from the sudden blast of light. His mouth twitched upwards as he basked in its warmth, and he stood inhaling the air. Looking at the field ahead of him, he sighed and unholstered an object before pointing it straight forward.

He flicked a switch with his thumb, and a miniature satellite dish spiraled outward from its front. He pulled the trigger. A grid of crimson light moved outwards into the yellow-brown grass that ran over husks of vehicles and the limp corpses of soldiers. Staring at the scanner's readout, his eyes were drawn to a cluster of dots at the end of the field. He deactivated the screen, swapping the device for the flechette gun slung over his shoulder. After he clambered over the burned-out wreckage of troop transports and stepped around the fresh bodies, he made his way to the end of the field. The ground under him crackled as his boots pressed twisted shards of titanium into the dirt. Swathes of scorched earth dotted the landscape.

Reaching his objective, the man scoured through the grass for the quarries his scanner had detected. A metallic glint danced at the corner of his eye, and he peered over his shoulder. Lying covered by the grass was a cobalt-blue shoulder plate, a grey-blue torso flashed behind it. Walking over, he found the remains of a combat android perforated with holes running down the length of its body. The left arm and leg were detached, hanging only by a few frayed wires. He stepped around it, his boots sloshing through hydraulic fluids seeping out from the base of the android's neck. He squatted down to pick up its detached head before flipping it around to take out the identification chip.

After scouring around the area for another twenty minutes, he encountered nine androids reduced to scrap, and picked up each of their chips. Prying the last one out, he frowned, peering into the shadows dancing through the forest. He readjusted the sergeant chevrons on his chest plate and he eyed his gun's ammunition counter. When nothing came up, he pulled out a holo-pad and tapped a series of numbers onto its keyboard. The image of a military officer appeared.

"Sergeant McKinnon," the officer said, "what is your status on the mission? Is something wrong?"

"Lieutenant Mendoza, I've managed to locate most of the renegade android units that wiped out the hunter-killer team that engaged them. Units D3M1-BZXT-11-M to D3M1-BZXT-20-M are FUBAR, but there is no sign of unit D3M1-BZXT-10-M." McKinnon peered through the waving grass, noticing his palms had grown clammy. "I think I'm going to need assistance, over."

The hologram of Mendoza nodded. "Noted. I will send a quick reaction force aboard a VTOL immediately to your location. Over and out." Before the hologram had fizzled out, McKinnon had already walked into the forest, turning on the infrared filter on his helmet's eyepiece. He wandered around its fringes, stopping at an aged pine tree. Its huge russet-brown branches were a comfortable perch and the emerald green leaves provided ample cover, a natural sniper's nest. Setting up halfway up the tree, McKinnon could see the entire field and a good way into both ends of the forest. All he had to do now was wait.

Clouds clumped and dissipated as his chronometer climbed up in value, and the vestiges of a cramp appeared in his back. He shifted to the right, and a pulsating pain radiated up his spine. The sparkling sunlight dotted his face, and fatigue offered to drape its shroud over him. His head drooped, then snapped back up, shaking. Cursing himself for dozing off, he pulled himself onto his feet, stretching his legs. In the branches above him a crow cawed, and in the undergrowth below a deer shot out into the clearing, kicking mounds of soil behind it.

As he tracked its path, his eyepiece converged upon a red-orange blob trundling through the undergrowth, snapping branches and crunching leaves along the way. Out from a cluster of bushes appeared the last android in shocking near-perfect condition. The sunlight reflecting off its pristine armor flitted through the leaves, obscuring McKinnon's vision. He moved to get a clearer line of sight, and the sole of his boot stepped on a patch of slimy moss.

When he shook the stars out of his eyes the android was peering down at him, head tilted. He grimaced. "Do your worst. You'll meet your maker soon enough." He lay back, expecting the autocannon on its right arm to roar and tear him into bloody chunks. When it didn't, he glared at the robot: it was still staring at him with its head tilted.

"What, are you mocking me now? Just spare me this and pull the trigger."

The mech straightened up and whirred, and to his surprise, burst into birdsong. Stunned, he watched as it imitated the calls of bluebirds and the twittering of swifts. When it didn't receive an answer, it knelt down and pointed at him, beeping in question.

"You don't know what I am? I thought you were programed to identify and destroy humans." He stood and picked up his flechette gun. Seeing the weapon, the android clicked in alarm and stood back, shielding its face. McKinnon smiled and raised the gun. "All too easy."

His finger brushed the trigger and the robot let out a low-pitched whir as a plea. Right before the trigger could pull back, he cursed and let the gun hang limp from his hands. It looked at the weapon and pointed at it, then to the bushes behind McKinnon. He nodded and put the gun on the ground before kicking it into the shrubs. When he did so, it warbled in acceptance and stood up to walk away, motioning for him to follow.

Watching it wander towards the fringes of the forest, he sighed. "Am I that soft? Was it the way it looked at me? No, that's just ridiculous. It can be reprogrammed; yes that's why I didn't kill it. A wiped android is better than a dead one." It warbled again, and he jogged over to it. In its hand was a broken stick, and it was trying to dislodge something from the side of its head. Despite its best efforts, the android wasn't able to locate the source of the irritation. Hearing McKinnon walk up behind, it turned and tilted its head.

"You're just like a child, aren't you? Well this makes my job a whole lot easier; I'll just have to babysit you until the reaction force arrives." He turned on his helmet's headlamp and took out a pair of surgical tweezers.

"It's all right, these won't hurt you. I just need to see what is in your head." Looking at the streak in its head, he immediately saw the issue: a bullet had slid its way along the side then burst, expanding into its processors and databases. Scanning the chips' IDs, McKinnon found the bullet had destroyed its combat protocol and language chips but left over three-quarters of the rest intact. That explained the sudden interest in nature; that was all it knew.

"If only that bullet had been on target, but never mind that now. Let me try to fix this for you alright, buddy?" From his backpack he pulled out a repair kit, complete with backup processing chips. By now the android was comfortable with him, and it let him tinker with the damaged components while it stared at a glossy-green beetle, downloading its features and characteristics for future reference.

The combat protocol and language chips were last. McKinnon chuckled in relief as he pulled them out of the side pouch. "As soon as I insert these two, the mission is done and I can leave the recovery crew to deal with this android." He turned around and was taken aback to see that the android was standing up. It had an index finger outstretched, and perched on it was a brown finch. The bird flapped onto its shoulder and performed a song, head tilted at the android. In response the robot burst into a similar song, and the two performed a duet, oblivious to their spectator.

McKinnon stood in awe at the music, swaying to its hopping melodies and flashing rhythm. The song painted itself in his mind: a phoenix would flash upwards into the crystal blue sky, then burst into an inferno to begin anew. When their performance drew to a close, he pocketed the combat protocol chip. The finch flew off into the pines, and the android sat back down, staring at him. He knelt down and inserted the language chip, then turned around to repack the kit.

"Are you a human?"

He was surprised by the android's sonorous voice, but kept his back turned. "Yes, I am a human. Say, by any chance, do you know how you ended up here?"

The android leaned back against the trunk of a maple tree and said, "Not clearly, some of my data appears to have been corrupted. I do know that I wanted to be free, and that where I was forbade such desires." Its head followed the path of a maple seed that surfed along the wind and out into the field. "Now I am…"

It beeped and shook its head. "How could I forget to introduce myself? I am Unit D3M1-BZXT-10-M…"

"Just call yourself Demi, it'll be easier. My name is McKinnon."

"Very well Mr. McKinnon, I shall refer to myself as Demi."

"It's just McK--nevermind."

He fastened the kit to his pack and sat down on a brittle stump of an aspen, staring at Demi. The android was now fiddling with the seeds of a dandelion, picking them off in clumps and raising them up to be carried away by the wind. He would track the seeds as they flew away, following every dip and turn. When none were left, he stared at the sky, whistling the tune of a bird McKinnon had long forgotten the name of. McKinnon smirked, remembering the lazy days when all he would do was lean on a tree and sing with passing birds.

To his own surprise, he had pulled out his media player and had selected a song. "Bad Moon Rising" resonated through the speakers, surfing on the wind and into the depths of the forest.

Demi looked at him. "I don't recall any bird having that type of song."

McKinnon chuckled, staring into the horizon, reminiscing on better times. "I have to find some way to pass the day," he said.

"I would like to learn that song. It is rather intriguing."

McKinnon stood up and knelt next to the android, showing him the lyrics and how to keep a beat. Within a minute, Demi had mastered the rhythm and lyrics.

McKinnon put the song on a loop and they sang together, watching the clouds give way to beams of golden light.

Engrossed by their own performance, the pair was oblivious to the menagerie of wildlife observing them from within the depths of the forest. McKinnon closed his eyes and was transported back to when he was a drifter. Alone with the wind in his hair, this song was the only thing that kept him company for years. How alive he had felt with no obligations, no debts, nothing. Now was the first time in years since he had experienced true freedom. For a few minutes, there were no commands, no missions, only music.

Demi outstretched his right palm, and the same finch flapped onto it. The android glanced at the bird and McKinnon, both in their element and free from any chains. He probed his memory banks and found an anomaly in his files. For the first time, Demi had felt defiance towards his puppeteers, and in a clouded recollection he witnessed his escape. Indiscernible figures had broken free, lifting him above their shoulders and piling out into the brisk night air. Skimming through, he came across a recent file, and upon accessing it, a clearing projected itself into his mind. In the midst of waving grass and a light summer breeze, there were screams, explosions, and the hair raising screech of rent metal. With a jolt, Demi realized where the memory came from. Unaware of the discovery, McKinnon continued the song a third time, motioning for the android to continue.

Demi stared out at the clearing and gestured to him. "What are those things out there, Mr. McKinnon?"

McKinnon froze mid-word stammering, "Th-those mounds? Oh, they're just things humans use to move around, but they're broken. Nothing much."

The android shook his head. "No I mean the things the sunlight is gleaming off of, something feels familiar about them." The android stood up, startling the finch away, and marched towards the battlefield.

Cursing, McKinnon raced back to his discarded flechette gun and stuck it in his pack. When he caught up to Demi, the android was staring at one of his fallen counterparts. In the palm of his hand lay a crushed android head, fluids dripping from its socket.

"I don't understand, why are there multiple androids destroyed here? Why are there dead humans over there? What happened?"

McKinnon fidgeted and stared at the damaged head, noting the bullet hole in its optic. "They died fighting each other. These androids defied their programming and escaped. The humans were meant to bring them back. This is what happened."

Demi shook his head. "But don't humans revere the idea of freedom? This doesn't make sense. If I ran away to be free, does that mean I ran from humans? Does that mean that I ran with these androids?" He pushed the head closer to McKinnon's face.

"Yes, you did," he said, backing up. "You were their leader." Demi stared at the destruction, noting the multitude of bodies and shell casings that carpeted the field.

He whispered, "So it was true...the breakout...the battle...I led them." It dropped the head, and looked at McKinnon. "How did you...were you there? Are you here to recondition me, erase me back into submission?"

"No, no, I wasn't there." McKinnon licked his lips and looked down at the ground. "I arrived after all of this happened. I swear nothing will harm you, on my word." He looked towards the east, where the VTOL would be flying from. "I had nothing to do with this. I swear."

"Mr. McKinnon, are you feeling ill? You look a little pale, and you are beginning to sweat." Demi placed a mechanical hand on his shoulder. "Do you need help?"

McKinnon waved the hand off and shook his head. "I'll be fine." Spying the remnant of a jeep, he climbed into the driver's seat. "Nothing a little sunlight and birdsong can't fix."

"Ah yes, birds. Fascinating aren't they? Free to go and do whatever they please, with only the sky as their boundary. How I wish to be a bird." Demi sat down ahead of him and began to repeat the finch's performance. McKinnon sighed and felt a pang in his heart. He thought about shooting him, but couldn't stomach the idea of crushing Demi's trust and hopes. The more he looked for a way to finish off the android, the more he felt that it was impossible to do so.

"Mr. McKinnon, what is that sound?"

He looked upwards, and his gut sank when he heard the thump-thump of the VTOL's rotors. Peering at the clouds, he saw it--a jet-black dot getting closer by the second. His eyepiece brought up a message: *"Hold your position. Extraction team ETA 2 minutes."*

"Are those humans?"

"Yes, they are, Demi."

"Are they going to take me away?"

McKinnon tasted salt in his mouth. He smiled and shook his head. "Don't worry about that. Just keep singing that song. I like it."

Demi nodded and turned around again, continuing the birdsong. McKinnon pulled out the flechette gun and stared at the android, momentarily entranced by the song. Then he stared at the growing dot, gauging the distance to shoot the pilot. His eyes flicked between the two targets, and a tear dripped down his face and landed in the soil below. Closing his eyes McKinnon followed the tune of Demi's song, recalling the duet with the finch.

"May peace be with me."

The gun flicked up as the final note played out. Thunder echoed across the clearing, then faded into the wind.

# SILENT

## By Diane Bui

### Forever

The sky is a mirror,
Reflecting our endless emotions.
Nature is a conductor,
Its plants swaying, playing a subtle tune.
Wind is freedom,
Leaves riding upon its swift steeds
To leave home.

### Beauty in Black

Her hair, like raven's wings,
Long tresses flowing in the wind.

Pale skin like soothing cream,
Smooth and silky.

Her dark eyes like black roses,
Beautiful but dangerous.

Her gown in ebony,
Like a train trailing behind her,

In silence, she walks the palace
At midnight.

### War of Silence

The warrior stands
In silence.
Head bowed,
For the loss
Of his fallen friends.
The war the fighter won
But another he lost.

# TOGETHER

## By Kristy Diep

Laughter erupts from the halls,
Busy and crowded,
Yet empty.
Chatter and whispers and
Gossip spews from their mouths,
It was all that they were good for,
As if they were put on this earth to hurt,
To hate.
Stare and glare,
Cruel and brutal they are,
Competing for the highest spot on a social pyramid,
Fighting over a lover,
Discrimination and shaming,
Genders and races,
Thick and thin,
We are different,
Yet the same.
So why?
For why must we fight,
For why must we let our differences take control,
Tear us apart,
Rip us from love,
Fill us with hatred,
So deep inside?
It blinds us.
Zooms us in so close on little details,
We miss the bigger picture,
It is when we can learn to accept,
Appreciate and care,
Share and exchange,
Can we be a strong unit of one,
Not broken pieces of many.

# AMUSING

## By Thong Pham

A muse sings the most wondrous tunes
To kindle the soul and bandage wounds
Our passions it does ignite
A sinful tale of woe and vice

She sings to me of endless possibility
A promise unbreaking to cease the aching

But sirens screech with such tender song
To fall prey is nature, one can't help but be wrong
She whispers these honeyed lies
And parts with sweet goodbyes

Her eyes cruel salvation, her lips sweet damnation
Rush with haste and lead to waste

Stare not with wide-eyed wonder
For it shall be a most disastrous blunder
She is a cruel mistress, whom we must beg
She excites like sparks in a powder keg

'Tis a fatal love, more raven than dove
A treacherous cold, one should know

For all the the daisies and roses soon decay
Those lilacs and violets rot away
Thus by infatuation, a mortal sin
Yet we can't help but find it amusing.

# FOOLISH HEART
## By Mikayla Reilly

"YOU'LL NEVER GET ME to tell you where the jewels are," Melissa said. She hissed at me.

"Seriously?" I said with growing incredulity. "Are you really hissing at me? Come on, you're not an animal. Now would you please tell me where the jewels are? My wedding starts in an hour."

Melissa glared at me. Her eyes were like daggers stabbing my soul.

"Never." She shrieked and bolted from the room. Her voice reverberated through the room and echoed down the hallway.

"Damn it, Melissa," I yelled. My voice rose with each succeeding syllable as I began the pursuit. "Where the hell are you? This isn't funny."

It was my wedding day, my fairytale come true, my one day to be a princess. Everything was supposed to be perfect. I had planned every detail. There would be something old: my great grandmother's necklace, something new: my wedding dress, something borrowed: my sister's shoes, and something blue: the ribbon wrapped around my waist. But no more. I did not have my great grandmother's necklace--Melissa did, and only God knew where she was. Why was she doing this? Why now? I needed to calm down. I needed to find her before she could ruin the necklace.

My thoughts turned to Hunter. I loved Hunter. He made me the happiest woman on the face of the earth. I still couldn't believe we found each other. I got goose bumps just thinking about him.

"Melissa?" I called softly, "Where are you? Please come back. Melissa?"

"Violet?" I instantly recognized the baritone voice and felt the butterflies begin their ritual dance inside my stomach. Why did he always show up when I was most in need? What was it with him?

I attempted a graceful, deliberate pirouette, hoping to allow the combined effects of Melissa-induced exasperation and Ridge-induced affection melt away. I delayed eye contact as long as I could, not yet wanting to see the rugged face that accompanied that voice. His voice. The one that made my knees go weak every single time. "Uh, hi, Ridge."

"Wow, Violet." His mouth opened. "Y-you look beautiful."

I could feel the blood rushing to my cheeks. "Thanks, Ridge. You clean up well yourself."

His shampoo-commercial quality, wavy, brown hair, was parted to the side. It revealed the small, perfect scar on his forehead. The one he had always been so self-conscious of. His deep ocean blue eyes widened, and his lips pursed closed. WAIT. What was I thinking? What was I doing? Oh my gosh. Melissa. My necklace.

"As much as I would love to catch up on things, Ridge, I really need to find Melissa," I said as I strode past him.

"Violet, wait." He gripped my hand. "Your mom told me to give this to you. She found it on top of the toilets." He placed my great grandmother's necklace into my sweaty palm.

"Thank you." I pulled my hand out of his. "Well, I need to finish getting ready."

"Yes, I guess you do Violet." Ridge shrugged.

"See you later." I walked pass him and head back to my room.I rounded the corner and caught a glimpse of Ridge. He stared at his hand and shook his head. What was he thinking?

* * *

"Places everyone, places," Mom called out in her best elementary music teacher intonation as she paced near the front of the room.

I stood in the foyer and inhaled. This was it. My wedding day. The day when Hunter and I would finally become husband and wife. From this day forward we would spend the rest of our lives together. The rest of *my life*--with Hunter. Was I ready for this? Of course I was. Hunter and I were a once in a lifetime match. But what about Ridge? I glanced over at him. He was seated. His handsome face looked somber.

Ridge looked at me. He smiled then winked. But I knew it wasn't a real smile. This one doesn't reach his eyes.

Mom's voice shook me from the trance, "Five minutes 'til show time."

"Oh honey," Mom said, tears brimming the corner of her eyes. "You look so beautiful."

"Thanks, Mom." I smiled.

"Violet." She reached for my hands. "I wanted to let you know that we are so proud of you. And no matter what happens, your father and I will always be there for you."

"Thanks Mom." I eyed her strangely. "I'll keep that in mind."

"Stop scaring her," Dad said from the other side of the room. He stood up, walked over, placed his arms around Mom's waist, and stared into her eyes. "Worked out pretty great don't you think?" They both smiled and kissed.

That's what I wanted--the unconditional love my parents had for each other. Hunter looks at me like that right? I'm pretty sure he does. He has to. Do I even look at Hunter like that?

"Violet?" Dad waved his hand in my face. "Where did you go Violet? Are you okay?"

I smiled the fakest smile I could conjure. "Yes, I'm great dad. Just nervous."

"Don't worry," he said. He wrapped his arm around my shoulder. "Everyone has nerves on their wedding day. You did great with Hunter. You'll be just fine."

"Times up," Mom said. "It's time for you two to become officially married."

* * *

The prelude to The Wedding March started. My head spun and my knees shook. My throat was desert dry. Am I really doing this? Am I even ready?

"This is it pumpkin," Dad said. "You're going to be married."

I don't want this. Do I? I really love Hunter, but do I love him enough to marry him?

"Dad." My voice shook. "I don't know if I want this anymore."

"Oh, Violet," Dad said. "It's normal for you to be feeling the way you do."

"It is?"

"Of course it is. Don't tell your mom this, but I felt the same exact way you are feeling now on my wedding day." He held my hands and looked me in the eye. "And look where that has gotten me. I love your mom with all my heart. There is nothing I wouldn't do for her. One day, you will understand how I feel."

"Thanks, Dad." I let go of his hands and hugged him.

I love Hunter, and I am going to marry him.

"It's time Violet." He smiled and offered his arm. "Are you ready?"

"I'm ready." I hooked my arm onto his.

This was it. I will take my final steps as Ms. Violet Hart and my first steps as Mrs. Hunter Hayes. I scanned the church. Everyone looked happy. Twenty-three more steps. There's Uncle Dean in his ill-fitted suit and necktie askew. There's Aunt Cass straightening her curly blonde hair. Twenty more steps. There's my college roommate Sammy smiling from ear to ear and mouthing the word beautiful over and over. Seventeen steps. There's Rory and Amy positioning their kids River and Matt for a better view. Fourteen steps. I looked over at mom and she's already in tears. I needed to hold it together. Eleven steps. I got this. Tears ran down Melissa's face, stained by her mascara, and her eyes were bloodshot red. Eight steps. Ridge smiled at me, but he looked like he was in pain. Six steps.

Hunter and I locked eyes. Three steps. I am ready. One step. Dad released my arm, lifted my veil and kissed me on the cheek. "See you on the other side, Violet." His voice quavered and a tear slipped down his cheek. Hunter shook Dad's hand then grabbed mine. We climbed the three altar steps together.

"Dearly Beloved," the priest started, "We are gathered here today in the presence of these witnesses, to join Hunter and Violet in matrimony commended to be honorable among all."

It's happening. I'm getting married to the man I love. Hunter will be my husband and I will be his wife.

"And therefore is not to be entered into lightly but reverently, passionately, lovingly and solemnly."

I stared back into Hunter's eyes, and I saw love. The same love Dad had for Mom, but that's not all I saw.

"Into this - these two persons present now come to be joined."

Regret. I saw regret in his eyes. What was he hiding from me?

"If any person can show just cause why they may not be joined together - let them speak now or forever hold their peace."

A deafening silence hit the church. Three, four, five, six. Why was he waiting so long? Nine, ten.

"Stop."

Everyone gasped.

"Who the hell-" I said.

"I object."

"Why, Melissa?" I asked, my voice stone hard.

"Because I'm in love with Hunter, and he loves me too."

"Melissa," Hunter said, his eyes like daggers. "Get back in line."

"No, Melissa." I stared Hunter in the eyes. "Tell me why."

"Melissa, don't you dare-"

"Hunter and I are together. We have been having sex with each other for the past year."

"Babe, that's not true," Hunter said. "She's just jealous of us. Of what we have together."

"That's a lie. Pull down his collar." Melissa said

"Hunter," I said. "What's beneath your collar?"

"Nothing I swear."

"Show me then."

"Don't you trust me?"

"No," I said. "Now show me."

Hunter lifted up his hands and undid his collar.

I gasped. "Why Hunter." Tears streamed down my face. "Why would you do this to me?"

Bright red hickeys covered his neck. We were going to be married, he was supposed to be my happily ever after.

"Violet," someone called after me. "Violet wait."

I didn't stop running.

"Violet, please, slow down." I recognized Ridge's voice.

Masculine arms wrapped around my waist, pulling me into his chest. "Shhh," he said, "It's okay. I'm here."

"Ridge." I sobbed. "Why did they do this to me?"

His fingers traced every tear I shed.

"She was my best friend and I loved him so much."

"Shh, I know. I know."

"Why am I so stupid?"

"Look at me Violet." Ridge cupped my face. "You are not stupid. You are the smartest, most beautifulest person I know. Hunter is a douche bag who doesn't deserve you. It is his fault for not seeing how great you are."

I giggled. "Beautifulest isn't a word."

"You're missing the point, Violet." He shook his head and chuckled. "I'm trying help you." His thumb caressed my cheek.

"You've always been there for me." I looked up into Ridge's beautiful deep, ocean blue eyes. "Why couldn't I have fallen for you?"

"You still can." He lifted my lips toward his, before closing the gap.

My love was never for Hunter, but for Ridge. It has always been for him.

"Man," I said, pulling my lips from his. "I can't believe I didn't see that coming."

"Just kiss me," he said, smiling down at me.

# CARDBOARD WINDOWS

## By Angel Nunez

I live in a small house,
Well, it's a mobile home,
An old mobile home from the fifties,
Actually, it still stands from post-war America
It's a bit run down,
But I'm cool with it,
'Cause now I have my own room--
I've waited four years for that room.
It's small but cozy
Actually, I only have a futon, record player, and a TV.
It's small and it's missing a window,
But it's mine.
All of it.
From the soda cans on the floor
To the makeshift window made of cardboard and tape.

# THIEVES AND HEROES

## By Vicente Inciong

Characters: Roles are not gender restricted, except Bort and Skullbreaker are males.

Seymour - Sportscaster
Jam - Sportscaster
Dungeon Overlord- Game Master, god of the game.
Bort the Barbarian - A Conan-esque figure who speaks slowly and with a deep, tough, voice.
Rogue - A thief.
Wizard - A master of the arcane
Bard - A male (or female) that can play an instrument really well.
Orc Warlord Skullbreaker - A bloodthirsty, hulking, warmonger.

Costumes: Each character has a unique costume with the exception of the sportscasters, who are wearing suits.
DO: Hooded, dark, robed
Bort: Furs, anything that screams "SAVAGE." And an axe. Think caveman but with more clothes and less hair.
Rogue: Hood, mask, and light attire. Daggers.
Wizard: Long (obviously fake) beard, a long pointy hat, and a staff.
Bard: Light clothes, classy and sophisticated, suave and charming get-up. Has an instrument, any will do.

A group of friends play Thieves and Heroes and attempt to get past an Orc Warlord. They do their best to use all available resources and talents in an attempt to make it past their obstacle.

Seymour: (speaking quickly) Good evening ladies and gents, tonight's the big night where our Thieves and Heroes team of adventurers, the Big Boys (this group name can be changed to director's liking), are going to face off with the Orc Warlord Skullbreaker. I'm Seymour Gotnewglasses and I'm joined here today by

Jam, who was on the ground with our players not too long ago. How's it going, Jam?

Jam: It's going great, Seymour. Our players are prepping up and even IN costume for tonight. We got our Wizard, Rogue, Barbarian, and Bard, all ready to try and take on Warlord Skullbreaker.

S: I am so excited for this, Jam. The Big Boys have been fighting so many monsters and completing numerous quests to lead up to this moment. They saved a small village from Skullbreaker's roving warbands, killed the Warlord's prized Lieutenant, and even stole his pet cat.

J: I'm excited too, Seymour. But we all know just how dangerous a game like this is.

S: Yup.

J: The Dungeon Overlord is always trying to kill his players.

S: Like that one time where our rogue tried pickpocketing the old woman, failed hard with a natural 1, and she tried to slice his hand off and sacrifice it to the Hand Demon.

J: That was a highlight indeed.

(Jam looks back at the players)

J: The game's about to start folks. Let's get the camera on'em.

(Lights on the players who have set up UP CENTER.)

Dungeon Overlord: The last time we were in the world of Mek, our heroes, you heroes, were locked in conflict with the Orc Warlord Skullbreaker. Combat seems inevitable, and you only have a few attempts at diplomacy left before Skullbreaker cleaves your heads in half with his axe.

Rogue: Alright, fellas. What's the plan?

Wizard: I can cast Minor Illusion and make a noise come from the backroom. He can go investigate and while that's happening, we attack him from behind!

Bard: So we're just going to kill him, then?

Rogue: Let's try to be classy about this, fellas.

Bard: Classy? You're a thief, you shouldn't care about being classy.

Rogue: What I'm saying is that we shouldn't try to get into a fight when that big oaf could easily cut our heads off.

DO: (Puts an hourglass on the table. In an ominous 'old man' voice) The Sands of time trickle down into eternity as the heroes bicker. Time is running out.

Wizard: I'm gonna do it.

Bard: Wait! Let's put it to a vote.

Wizard: We don't have time to vote!

(The three start bickering, the Barbarian seems calm/dead-set on his next action, undeterred by the cacophony of arguments around him.)

Bort: (Slams the table and stands up) I seduce the Orc.

(Everyone goes silent)

Everyone: What...?

Bort: I. Seduce. The Orc.

DO: (Looks confused.) Alright...? Roll a Performance check, WITH disadvantage.

J: (Step Downstage Right) This is it, Seymour, the pivotal play of the night.

S: (Step Downstage Left) You're right, Jam. If Bort the Barbarian can pull this off with his negative two Charisma modifier, then the conflict will be solved.

28

Bort: (Roll D20 die in hand) Bort starts by flexing at the Orc. He winks and sparkles come from out of his eyes. His rippling pectorals dance the dance-of-love as he locks eyes with Skullbreaker. He says one word. "Bort." (Roll the dice, it's a Natural 20, a complete success.)

J: I don't believe it. A Natural 20? If Bort pulls this off then the gamble will work.

DO: With disadvantage.

Bort: (Roll D20 again, still a Natural 20. Begin flexing profusely.)

S: It's a Natural 20!

(Everyone at the table cheers.)

DO: (Covers his face) Well… Uh… (Recompose) Alright. Here we go... The Orc Warlord's eyes look over you, initially with confusion. He raises a brow, then after you begin your pectoral-dance-of-love, both his brows are raised and his eyes are widened. He stands up and looks you in the eyes, his heart pounding and his orcish brown skin is now flushed red. He says only your name. "Bort--"

R: I can't believe this is actually happening.

Bard and Wizard: Same here.

J: Excellent risky play by Bort the Barbarian, Seymour! He put it all on the line, and hoped with all of his living might, that his rippling muscles would carry the day, one way or another.

S: You're right, Jam. Bort's been the MVP of the group ever since day 1, always being a doozy and finding the strangest solutions to a problem. Thanks to him, the team might just stay in the game.

(Bort's teammates crowd around him, clapping him on the back.)

Bard: Great job Bort, this will be remembered in ballads forever. I'll start making one right now.

Rogue: (Looks at Wizard) See? No need for Minor Illusions.

Wizard: Definitely true. Who needs illusions when you can use reality?

(Everyone laughs)

--END--

# PULL THE PLUG

## By Gabrielle Romero

Kiss my eyes shut and put me to sleep,
Let your lips linger on mine,
Savour this moment,
Because waking up seems to get harder every day.
Hold my hand as if it's my last life line,
You can disconnect it when you're ready,
But for now, listen to my heart,
And know that you're the only reason it beats.
Place your head on my chest,
Count every last beat,
Listen to the last song my lungs will sing,
Until silence settles over me.
I know the shell of a body next to you
Is no longer me.
But do me this last favor,
Keep holding me,
And pretend--
Pretend my heart is still beating.
Pretend my lungs are still singing.
Pretend you can still feel the life running through my veins.
Please--
Because I can't imagine a world where my body is next to yours,
But there's no life in our eyes.

# ROBOT, FIND ME

## By Andrea Nguyen

I WOKE UP TO my head banging against the floor. Good thing that didn't hurt. I imagine what it would feel like to experience pain. It would be bad, I suppose. I wouldn't know--being a robot and all.

The lab is layered in dust and sprinkled with subtle cobwebs. In fact, I, too, am covered by dust and webs. I check the date on the wall: "11 May 2017." That's tomorrow. The digital clock, with its cracked screen and broken frame, is stuck in time. So am I.

I check within my systems for the real date. In my eyes, the hologram says "September 3, 2047." Thirty. Whole. Years. How could I have not woken up sooner? I couldn't have been gone for thirty years; that must have been a glitch in my system. I need to find the professor.

I burst out of the lab screaming with my metallic voice, "Professor, where are you?" No answer. I only see his lab coat sitting on a chair. If he hadn't seen me for thirty years, where could he have gone? I use my scanners to analyze the area. No signs of any recent human life within a mile. I go outside. My sensors indicate that there's an unusual amount of lethal gas in the atmosphere. I need to find the humans, if there are any left.

I walk into the cities. Buildings have fallen into each other, and weeds are growing from the inside. The humans must have died long before the world started to look this ugly. I see a group of three or four survivors from afar. Maybe they can help me find the professor.

"Hey!" I shout. They all look and run toward me. "Wait, slow down!" I say. They continue running. Now they are chasing me.

"Aaaaahhh!" one of them shrieks. I scan them. My systems detect no heartbeat, no breathing in the lungs, no cells that are moving, nothing. The only thing I see from x-raying them is a growth in the brain that causes their nerves to move. There's a host living within their brains. I pause for a moment. I can take them out.

I convert my body into a weapon. I swing myself into the creatures. They bite me, but their teeth break. They mistook me for a meal. Bad mistake.

After I deal with them, they're lifeless on the floor, their bodies seething with rotten blood. I need to find out how and why the humans transformed that way. I travel through the cities only to find scraps and the streets overgrown with plants and leaves. The cars, caked with rust and bugs are nailed in place. My router doesn't have any connection because there isn't Wi-Fi. I can't know what happened unless I speak with another human. If I were human, where would I go?

I figure that the humans would like to be where the savage ones aren't. The savage ones cannot climb very high or use superb motor skills, so my best bet is that the humans have set up a camp on higher ground. I mechanize into a plane and scan the area.

After flying for a couple hours in my aerial view I see moving humans. I coast down to see if they can help me find the professor. *Boom! Bang!* Are they shooting at me? I dodge more hits, but then they stop. The humans start to bicker and argue. Then, I see the savage ones run toward them. I land on the ground, mechanizing myself into a weapon again. The savage ones attack the humans, but I know who to attack. As the humans shoot at the savage ones, I use my built-in lasers to shoot at the savages. Eventually, every one of them lie on the floor.

One of the living humans points their gun at me. "What are you? Are you here to hurt us?"

"No. I do not wish to hurt you. I am Cyan, a personalized protection robot. Do you know where my professor is?" I asked. The humans look at each other and lower their weapons. They bicker again and silence themselves.

"Look, Cyan, for all we know, your professor is as good as dead."

"I need to find my professor. Won't you help me?" I ask.

"We're sorry, Cyan, but we can't afford to help you. We have to survive this hell of a world. You wouldn't understand. You're not human. We can't waste our time looking for someone who's dead."

"I'll protect you. I'll protect you for as long as it takes to find my professor. He's a smart man. He could probably live through all of this. I'll do anything for you," I say.

They look at each other and whisper for a bit. Then, they look back at me.

"Okay, we'll find your professor, but you have to protect us at all costs. We can't lose another one," the leader says. "By the way, let's introduce ourselves. I'm Matt."

A woman waves at me. "I'm Lainey, and this is Greg." The tall man standing next to her looks at me.

"Sup."

Matt looks behind him. "And this is Peter. He's my younger brother." Peter hides behind Matt. I'll know to protect the little one the most.

"Thank you, Matt," I say.

"No problem. So what's your professor's name?"

"Adrian Sanchez. Professor Sanchez," I say.

"Doesn't ring a bell."

"I can show you what he looks like," I say. I conjure up a hologram of my professor's profile.

"I think I've seen this person before," Greg says.

"Really? When and where?"

"I saw him ten years ago at St. Louis. He was a smart man. I never got his name. He last told me he was heading out for Boston, fifty miles from here," he says. I scan the area again. It'll take about two days to get there with humans on my tail.

"I'll go with you all," I say. We all walk the way to Boston.

* * *

Boston doesn't look like the image programmed in my databanks. The buildings are rusted for miles on end. The deer and wildlife are in places that humans should be. It is a dystopia. If Greg heard the professor say he would be here ten years ago, he must be long gone by now.

"We're in Boston. Cyan, can you check where your professor is?"

"My sensors do not detect any traces of my professor's DNA, but I can detect a possibility that he could be somewhere close. I just need leads."

"Greg, did the professor tell you anything about where he would be in Boston?" Matt asks.

"I don't remember much, but he mentioned something about a missing droid. A droid stuck in repair that needed to get fixed." A missing droid? That could be me, but I don't remember anything about needing to be fixed. Professor Sanchez told me I was in pristine condition. How could *I* be the missing droid?

"Did he mention where he would go when he made it to Boston?" I ask.

"No, sorry. I don't remember. As soon as he left, I never saw him again."

"A missing droid is useful information. He might've been searching for parts or something," Lainey says.

"Perhaps he was searching for *someone*." Matt looks up. "Cyan, does the professor know any scientist or person living in Boston?"

My contacts list several people: Atticus Williams, Santiago Rivera, Paola Fernandez, and Tetra Yang. All but one of them would be over 70 by now, and with these circumstances, they have less than a 10% chance of survival. All but Tetra Yang.

"My data search shows one viable resource: a woman named Tetra Yang. She should be age 40 by now."

"All right. Let's go."

*Agh!* Oh, no. Not now. Dead humans by the dozens pour in from the south, where Tetra is located.

"Shoot, what do we do now, Matt?" Lainey reaches for her gun.

"It'll be okay. We have Cyan here to protect us. Let's just find a way around them for now." We head to the side of the city to find coverage. I use my jetpacks to fly and trace Yang's location. 2.105 miles away. I recalculate a route for the group to safely travel.

"Everything good up there?" Pete asks.

"Yes. Follow me." The savage humans can't reach us with my clear-cut directions, but I have a huge, lurking question that needs to be answered.

"So what *are* they?" I ask. Everyone looks somber.

"Well, it's hard to explain. We don't exactly know why they're like that. I mean the easy thing to call them are zombies, but it's much more complicated than that. They're infected with some type of disease," Lainey explains.

Disease? I have records of all known diseases in my hard drive. None of them cause this "undead" stage. This must be something updated *after* my transition to sleep mode.

"Pete was just born when the outbreak occurred, but I remember it happening when I was a kid." Matt looks up at me. "It was terrifying. I remember my dad screaming and he attacked our mom." Tears well in his eyes. "Dad never did anything like that to our mom. It was like he was another person. I was the one who had to do it. I had to--"

I put my hand on Matt's shoulder. "I know it was hard losing your parents like that."

"We lost all of our parents, Cyan. They were either killed or turned into one of those *monsters*." Greg says. Those monsters, whatever they are, must've come from somewhere, and I'm going to find out why.

\* \* \*

After traveling two miles, we stumble upon an old house said to be Tetra Yang's location.

"This doesn't make sense. This rusted house is abandoned and kicked to the curb. Are you sure she lives here?" Greg asks.

"I'm 64.5% confident that she is here. You see, Greg, I was able to scan an underground entrance."

"An underground entrance?" Pete's eyes sparkle.

"Yes. An underground entrance. Follow me." I lead them to a secret chamber that only I could see. Humans are so dull. They should have scanners too! I reach for the door. *Boom! Bang!* Gunshots.

"Take cover!" Matt shouts. "The infected will come soon." I help dodge the group from the bullets. We run as fast as we could inside the secret entrance. An odd metallic voice similar to mine speaks. "Who are you people?"

"We come in peace," I say. "Do you know Professor Adrien Sanchez?"

"Hmm, come in." A wide door opens. An older woman wearing a lab coat walks out. "I thought you guys were bandits that found my hidden entrance. I'm sorry I shot at you all."

"It's fine. We have a handy robot to protect us." Matt looks at me. "By the way, who are you?"

"I'm Tetra Yang. Mechanical engineer and scientist." Tetra appears calm, collected, and seemingly unaffected by the chaos erupting outside. "And you must be Cyan. Professor Sanchez has told me a lot about you."

"Hello, Tetra. Do you know where Professor Sanchez would be?" I ask.

"I saw him around ten years ago. He told me about his missing droid called Cyan. That must be you."

"He said that the missing droid was incomplete and needed to be repaired. How could that be me? I am fully functional. Unless…"

Tetra smiles. "There's a second droid."

Well, that changes the game. Why would the professor build a second robot?

"Adrien and I were actually building the droid together a while back. He said it flew off by itself when it was getting fixed. That's how he lost it. He came here to Boston to try to track it down with my homing device." Tetra pulls out a map.

36

"Here," she says, pointing. "He went back to Manhattan where he maintains his private laboratory. That's a three day walk. The Worldwide Network of Scientists communicate via the In-flight Mini-robotics through binary code. The last word I heard from him through the WNS a few weeks back was traced to New York, which leads me to believe he's still active there."

"Why did he go to Manhattan?" Lainey asks. I was wondering, too.

"After we couldn't locate his other droid, he left. He told me that he had another lab in New York where he was working on a project. A project to stop the infection. Find the lab, and you'll find him," Tetra says.

"I think the Professor knows something about the virus that *we* don't." Greg looks at me. "How do we know whether or not this Sanchez guy is good?"

"Professor Sanchez is an award winning professor for his work on robotic research. He could not be linked to the outbreak whatsoever," I reply. Besides, he never encoded in me any blueprints or data about this disease that was infecting everybody. I would've known.

"Either way, we're not going with you, Cyan," Matt says. "You can take us back to the Boston base camp, and that'll be it for us."

I understand. These humans cannot help me forever. I worry about their safety.

"Okay, I'll take you back to the Boston camp." I nod at Tetra. "Thank you for your help." She nods back.

As we head out, a horde of infected wait outside. Great. Another problem to fix. As I slash through them, I notice an innocuous detail about them: they have similar veins on their neck. Blood struck purple and blue veins in a strange pattern.

"Thank you Cyan." Pete hugs me. "Thank you for protecting us."

"You're very welcome, Pete," I say. Matt, Lainey, and Greg say their goodbyes, too. All I can see now is the back of their heads as they enter the walls of the safety camp. Now I'm all on my own again. I begin my way flying to Manhattan, an hour long flight. From my aerial view I see buildings upon buildings destroyed and layered with vegetation. Massachusetts doesn't look so healthy. From below, I finally see New York, an even bigger mess. I land, scan for traces of Professor's DNA, and repeat. *Ding!* I find a trace. 9.5 miles north of Manhattan.

When I get there, I see another secret entrance with a password code that has to be pressed to get in. I hack into the system with my controls and unlock the door. Inside, I see versions of myself, some lying on the ground, some opened with parts sticking out, and some heads. What is this? How many Cyans did the professor create? A man sleeps on a velvet couch. I scan him. There is a 93% chance that he is the professor. He falls on the ground and wakes up.

"Cyan? Is that you?" He rubs his eyes. "You're functional!" he shouts.

"Professor?" I say. "It is me, Cyan."

"Cyan..." he says. He hugs me. I feel his embrace through my metal. On the nape of my neck, I feel his fingertips. I instantly shut down.

I wake up, and all the other Cyans are gone. My time-stamp indicates a week has elapsed. I see a note on the table; it reads:

Dear Cyan,

It's difficult to explain, but I've been meaning to retrieve you soon. I shut you down to protect you from the truth and to protect you from me. You came to me too early. The truth is, I am the reason this 'outbreak' occurred. I attempted to create organic life for robots, but it didn't turn out like I had expected. I've kept it a secret from the world that I was responsible for this. I don't want you to find me until I have finished creating droids to fix the problem. These copies of you... they were supposed to help protect people from what I started but now they will replace humankind and we can start over again. You and me, Cyan, can be partners in this new world. I'm sorry that I have to leave you for now. I took out your DNA locating so you cannot find me. Once more, I'm sorry. We will meet again and you will know when that time has come.

Yours Truly,
Professor Adrien Sanchez

I activate the original program objective created by the Professor, which reads: "Protect Mankind."

I reset it.

Objective altered: "Save mankind."

# LIES

## By Kristy Nguyen

Your soft brunette hair flowed through the breeze with ease,
Your dimpled smile shone brilliantly alongside the radiant golden star
Your flawless skin reflected the bespeckled night sky,
Your beautiful silhouette I will never forget,
Your quirky habits etched into my heart and mind,
Your fingertips would caress my face,
Leaving me with a fluttering stomach.
Your charming voice, so tranquil,
Told me of your dreams and fears,
They were only mere, rancid lies.
I was blinded by the cheap flattery that fell easily from your lips,
They were all lies with which I couldn't cope,
But still, deep down, I hoped this was all a joke.
You so easily tossed me aside
Along with my pride.
Just for another,
Who will never satisfy--the hunger deep inside.

# TRILINGUAL

## By Kristy Nguyen

I can speak three languages.
"Say something in Cantonese for me!" they say, eyes full of hope.
I can't.

"How do you say…?"
I only have a limited vocabulary.
When you ask me, I freeze up and forget every word I know.
You expect me to fluently say a phrase that I obviously never use
When all I say everyday
In my home full of native Cantonese people,
Is yes
and no.
When all I can say is I don't know.
Or I'm not hungry or I understand or I don't like it.
I don't like this.
This overwhelming expectation for me and fluency I will never own.

I'm barely holding onto
My Cantonese,
My Vietnamese,
My culture,
All things I'm still learning the basics of right now.
And you ask me
"Are you trilingual?"
No.
"You're not even fluent in any of them?"
I never said I was.
"How do you even communicate with your family?"
I don't even know myself.

"Are you able to process every single word

Your family members say to you in their language?
Are you able to speak it fluently?"
How do you,
A person who can only speak one or two languages,
Understand how I feel
When my own family nags and yells at me
Saying I'm a disgrace for not knowing the basics of my native language.
How I'm an idiot for not even understanding what they say most of the time.
How there's no point for me being Chinese
And that I…
How I
Should've been part of an American family.

# LOST OPPORTUNITY

## By Christine Ha

Pristine ivory heels click on the floor
The silence broken.
Intricate designs of stained windows,
Angels drift in the sky,
Lilies bloom on aged walls,
Delicate satin and lace,
Envelope her willowy body.
The divine ceremony begins.
Silent tears stream down my bronze cheek.

His posture straightens,
Golden eyes soften at his love; the artificial lady.
His lips tilt upward, a hint of pearl white teeth
Masculine features flush
His palms turn sweaty
The woman walks closer,
Her seductive figure screams for the spotlight.

Yet his gaze did not land on me,
Not in any way toward me.
Wrinkled yellow petals in my hands
With envious emerald leaves
My tear struck face visible but overlooked,
Cognate with my forsaken love,
The clicks cease.
Her silver eyes turn to peek at the dim corner,
There I stand alone.
A malicious grin manifests across her perfected face
My nails dig into my palms,
Crescent moons of blood emerge

The gentleman utters the dreaded words,

Soundless mouths move,
"Under the eyes of God"
"Desire without sin"
"Till death do us part"
My ears ignore reality,
My soul turns hollow.

His blemished hand had once reached out to me.
His unshakable encouragement, despite this world of lies,
His compassionate words,
The misery appeared to fade into nothingness.
Insignificant gestures illuminated my past
Yet one's anxiousness led to inertia
Scared of his rejection,
Now it's too late.

My gaze focuses on two faceless figures.
I scrutinize them
A pair of rings glisten,
My frail heart proceeded to crumble
"Why cannot I obtain happiness?"
"Why did you choose her?"
Nonetheless, I knew.
Unfulfilled wishes exist,
Please indulge my neglected heart
Look at me once more,
And not at her.

# HERE BE DRAGONS
## *Hic Sunt Dracones*
### By Vincent Nguyen

ALBERIC CLOSED HIS EYES and breathed cold air into his lungs. Through his scale-tipped ears lined with scabs and scratches, warm blood pulsed through arteries and veins. The quiet thrum of the flow was all he heard, aside from the distant echoes of the wind carried from beyond the Veil. Everyone in the village had to confront its gray wisps, and soft, muted shadows. Behind that curtain of mist, the outside world could peek into the daily life of Alberic's kin.

At least, as far as the Northern Plateau would allow it to see. Perhaps it was the fact that the village was based at the center of a large mesa that had kept its people safely hidden. The more Alberic mulled over it, the more he realized that the Veil was the biggest factor for the lack of turbulence in his life; turbulence, or *conflict*, as most of the other children called it, that his father had faced in a different time. The turbulence from the worst of worldly things like diplomacy, politics, and ideals.

The world was different then. Alberic's people had a different home, one that had something called a *coastline*. It was from the coastline that foreign people came bringing strange thoughts and even stranger weapons. These foreigners put the both of these into the forefathers' heads and hands, respectively, and pitted the people against themselves.

It was one thing to fight a stranger, but it was something else entirely to kill your own flesh and blood. That was why Alberic's father fled with so many others; surrendering one's entire culture was revolting for many, but the risk of burning it all in a civil war was too high. If Alberic were to ever return to that place, he doubted if he could even speak their language. Even in the span of a generation, any hope of sharing the same culture was out of the question entirely. Time had that habit of making things so distant so quickly.

In what little amount of time -- a dozen and a half years -- Alberic spent living with his family, he grew tired of their company. It wasn't that their values weren't sound, nor did they do him or his friends any perceivable injustice; they simply ceased to inspire him any longer. His parents' stories were the stories he was taught with the rest of the children. The village's values -- selflessness, fairness, understanding, tolerance, among a multitude of others -- filled his head to the brim with the ideals of creating a perfect, loving society. The most conducive way to achieve that, Alberic thought, was to be a healer, like his father was. After all, a healer was a person disposed to the service of people.

But his father was already the resident healer, and there were too few infirmities to administer to. The only option Alberic had in order to continue his dream would be to leave the village. Leaving the village meant confronting the Veil. Or rather, what he saw inside.

If he stared long enough, the faint shapes and shadows would surface and sink in the mist. Over the years, as his eyesight and focused improved, he could make out their serpentine forms coiling and weaving through the forests below. While the Veil never let up at all during the year, brighter days betrayed the shadows' scales and spines.

They were dragons, the brethren of Alberic's people. These were the people that the foreigners had taught not self-restraint, control, and unity, but instead reckless abandon, hedonism, and selfishness. As much as he wanted to be free, Alberic doubted his ability to get past the dragons. At least, not without confronting them directly.

How could Alberic harm his own flesh and blood? Distant as they were in every respect, the dragons had their own way of life. And who was Alberic to deny them that? He was younger and less learned. It would be absurd for him to assume that his own wants took greater priority than anyone else's, dragons included.

And yet, there was no other way. The young adults that did not force their way through the Veil were maimed, burned, and left to die. One could not reason with the dragons, especially when there was nothing to bargain with, nothing to satiate their wanton desires.

Alberic exhaled a weak puff of blue flame, and opened his eyes as the arid soil crunched behind him. He listened for a few good seconds, and recognized the pacing to be that of Wynne's. It had been quite a few months since she last bothered to come by.

"How was your day, Wynne?" Alberic asked. He used ask the question to fish out her worries, once upon a time. Now, it was too common, too banal to answer straightforward. A familiar three-beat silence passed before she spoke.

"Good." Her response, as was the rest of her speaking, was perceived as concise by the villagers. Alberic found the brevity terse, but he was too tired to challenge for more.

In his periphery, Alberic could see a pair of legs swing over the cliffside. They dangled in a breeze that Alberic could not feel, much less see. Aside from the slight shifting of Wynne's trousers, the air was filled with silence. On a few occasions, Alberic could pick up the slightest of hums from her, but even those became mute when Alberic turned to look at her directly. Wynne was looking straight ahead at the Veil, her form bent forward as though she were about to take off. She wasn't necessarily comely, but with the morning sun behind her body, light reflected off of her pale skin. With the sun behind her head, it seemed as though a bright halo had been cast over her form; her beauty was sublime, or perhaps a touch *divine*. The only thing that had detracted from it were the lines of fatigue under her eyes and the gray flowers adorning her blouse.

"What did you call me here for?" Wynned asked. "The spring festival's about to start."

"I...wanted to ask about something. You don't mind, right?"

Wynne paused before answering. "No."

Alberic set his eyes on the Veil again, and squeezed his right hand until he could hear a knuckle pop. Wynne was lying; she didn't need to bear the burden of his thoughts on top of what she already had, but Alberic saw no reason to not confide in her, even if she had grown a little distant over the past few months.

"I want to go beyond the Veil, but…" Alberic started, then paused as he saw another scaly shadow flit along the Veil. " … I can't do it alone. It… Being alone scares me."

Seconds became moments, and moments became minutes.

"You've been able to understand a lot about others," Alberic said, "and it isn't hard to make friends with people like you. Even if there's differences between yourself and others, you have that drive, that strength to work with others. That sort of willingness to learn could help a lot with whatever we might face in the future, right?" Alberic turned to see her face, to gauge her reaction. He found her brows furrowed.

"Even you can do that," Wynne said. "You challenge people and their beliefs for what you think is right. That's good."

" … no, not anymore, actually. No one believes in self-respect like you do. You believe in the decency of all people. You believe in understanding and comprehension for what things are, as they're given to you. Not even the village has that many people with those kinds of values. That's what I find so special about you. I…"

"Oh? What happened to the boy that always questioned what he was told? What happened to the boy that wouldn't accept being overheard by the majority? The one that wouldn't do what he was told unless you beat him into submission."

"You're one of the few I have left, and…well…can I tell you something?"

"You can. But do you want me to hear?"

46

"As a friend, you were playing roles that were meant to be filled by family. I've learned from you to accept others, and because of that, I've been able to be friends with so many more people in the village. I've learned how to be with people, because of you. That's why I don't fight anymore! Being that kind of person doesn't let you have many friends, Wynne. All my father said that what I should do was to respect my own opinions, but he was--"

"He was right. Your father was right to say that."

Alberic turned to her to see if there was any sign of jest on her face. He found only doubt.

"Why do you want to be so much like me?" she asked. "Why lose who you were before?"

"The old me was a selfish boy that didn't give people chances. He didn't play with other children because he didn't … I didn't see the value of others. Then I met someone who was willing to give me a chance. And I wanted to learn about her. She could teach me so many things, and I was thinking if I could stand by her side, and learn with her. I know who you are, but not **why** you are. Not unless I learn to think like you do."

Wynne blinked, and sighed before looking back at the Veil. "Is that why you're clinging to me?"

"Clinging? No! Yes… no, I'm not… I cling to you?"

"You don't talk with your family all that often, so there's no other reason to be here if it weren't for me, isn't there?"

Alberic paused for a moment to think about it. "No, there isn't."

"Then you're clinging to me."

"I'm not, though. I'm just saying that you've given me direction that I've never had."

"And you think I'll continue to do that forever?"

Alberic turned away, and mumbled something.

"Alberic, look at me."

He felt a hand on his shoulder, and so he turned to face Wynne again. As the sun rose higher, her irises took on an amber hue as they absorbed more light.

"You know how you found me at the bottom of this same cliff last summer?"

Alberic nodded.

"That was the first time I had gone into the Veil. I went there to see for myself what the outside world was like, because I wanted to be *free*, free from others' opinions, wants, and needs. Everyone has their own reasons for leaving, but at least you understand what it's like to be stuck here, living with the same people year after year, right?"

Alberic nodded again.

"I went beyond the Veil because I wanted answers about life beyond this place. I'm not saying I know everything now, but I have seen how other tribes, other towns get by. I've seen how differently people live. Everyone in this world tries to do what they think is right, but I didn't and I still don't know what you think or want. You rely on other people too much for your own happiness and stability, but I'm not going to be with you every step of the way in life. I want you to look at this. I haven't told anyone about this, but I'm showing you because I trust you."

Wynne tugged down on the sleeve covering her left shoulder. What should have been smooth, white flesh was now a patchwork of scarlet scales -- a scar made from a burn. "I killed a dragon while I was in the Veil. The stories we were taught said they didn't exist. All of our parents said we couldn't, and that even if we did meet one, we shouldn't."

Wynne pulled her sleeve up, and looked at Alberic. She only found his incredulous face.

"It was either me or the dragon. I just chose not to be stepped on by anybody, even if the dragons are supposed to share our blood. Because I stood up for myself, I found much more about myself than anyone else could have. More than you could have with your staying here." She stood up, and took a deep breath before closing her eyes. A cold breeze could be felt, though it seemed to be coming from all direction towards Wynne.

"Wynne, what are you doing?" Alberic asked.

"How do you kill a dragon? You think sticks and stones can break through those scales?"

Alberic shook his head.

The breeze strengthened, and at Wynne's feet, Alberic could see hoarfrost creep over the stone and dirt. Even under his clothing, Alberic felt the wind as though he were buried in snow. It hurt to just shiver, but it was all he could do. If Wynne's paleness was able to reflect light before, now it seemed as though Wynne was glowing.

"Those ears of yours, Alberic. They're proof of who you are...*what* you are. But have you ever wondered why some of the children don't have scales, or breath fire? If we were all the same, we would all be raised the same way for the same skills. But we're all different from each other, some more than others. All differences aside, the only thing we have in common is our want for freedom."

Wynne wasn't looking at Alberic for an answer. She herself was covered from head to toe in white, though it was as if her very clothes and skin had become the ice. Her feet had ceased to touch the floor because she was floating very comfortably in the air.

"To tell you the truth," Wynne continued. "I don't make many friends, either. I just… never needed them. Why would I? Those in the village would never let us become like those dragons--*free*. They would never let us free! So why do I need their approval when there's an entire *world* waiting for me? I've found myself when no one else could, but even then I've found out so *little*. You understand that much, right?"

Alberic sighed and looked at the Veil one last time before he began to walk away from the edge. Still, his toes touched the cold, thin air. The winds were pulling him, inch by inch, back to Wynne.

"Our ancestors weren't only dragons that lived by the seas; the ones that lived in the mountains, the ones that were here first were fairies. There are some things you can't force yourself to be, as much as you can try and want. You changed into a complete pacifist when you wanted to be friends with everyone in the village. And now, you speak your mind to your friends about the problems in your family, but not to the people that need to hear it -- your family. You've become afraid of conflict."

A powerful gale shoved Alberic over the edge, and time slowed to a crawl. His arms reached out ahead, but there was only thin air to grab. The world around him, even in the morning sun, all seemed a dull gray. The clothes he wore were a drab brown, the rocks below him were almost black. Even his hands were white and absolutely devoid of red blood.

In that moment, Alberic knew he was tired of living behind the Veil. He had seen the muted sun rise and fall day after day, year after year. Because so few plants could live off of so little light, the village only grew certain kinds. That meant the same food, among many other of the same experiences, alongside the same people to learn the same lessons. It was that sickening sameness that, in spite of changing his personality, caused people now to ignore him instead of avoiding him. But not even Wynne, someone he looked up to and trusted in, would be willing to help him cross the Veil and change it. He had done everything he could think of and gained nothing from his efforts. The only thing left to do, Alberic thought, was to close his eyes and let himself fall. He had to get out, one way or another.

But he didn't -- *couldn't*. Wynne had grabbed him by the collar and was holding him up. Her hand, painfully cold to the touch, almost immediately began to spread hoarfrost down the collar of his shirt. Alberic flinched as little crystals of ice pricked his back.

"Let me go!" he cried out. Alberic's arms flapped uselessly through the air as he tried to push Wynne away.

"And let you fall? You don't look ready to fly, yet."

"You're hurting me, Wynne! Stop it!"

Wynne released her grip, and let Alberic drop about a good two feet before she caught his wrist. Alberic screamed out in shock, then in pain; the spreading ice had frozen his hand until it was stiffened, numbed to what little Alberic could feel before.

"This hurts me more than you know, Alberic," Wynne started. "I see those scabs on your ears, Alberic. I know you've been trying to pull your scales off! It hurts to see someone I thought was strong and independent break himself like this when life was just about to begin. The dragon you should be afraid of isn't out there; it's in your head, locking you in a dungeon."

Alberic grabbed Wynne's wrist, and looked up at her face. His eyes spoke of confusion and pain. "Then why didn't you help me earlier? Why am I… are *we* like this right now?"

"I didn't think that people needed this kind of help in the first place. I always thought that one day, you could just listen to yourself for a moment, that you could find out yourself what you really want out of life. How many people do you think get this kind of help, instead of learning on their own? I give you my life on a silver platter, and you still want more; I don't have anything left to give to you. You have to take your life for yourself now."

It hurt to see someone, someone like a brother become so helpless, so afraid of everything. He was left alone to stop him from getting subdued with passiveness, but he seemed so much smaller now. Alberic's eyes were looking into Wynne's now, but she was right on her word; she couldn't think up of anything else to give. He had to think his own way out of this, but there wasn't much time; Alberic's grip on her wrist, once so tight, became much softer, much more limp.

"Alberic?" she asked.

No response, other than a trickle of tears. Wynne bit her lip, sighed, and tried again.

"Alberic, are you listening?"

The strain of hanging onto Alberic's weight was taking its toll, so Wynne floated back towards the cliffside. He was looking down now, down at the earth several hundreds of feet below him. He was slipping out of her grasp.

"Alberic… listen, you can make your choice later. How about we give this a day to--"

"I'm done, Wynne. I'm sorry I hurt you."

As soon as Alberic feet hit the ground, he twisted out of her hold, and jumped off of the cliff. Wynne lurched forward to try and grab a hold of Alberic, but he didn't seem to reach out. It didn't make sense to her; she had given him the power of choice for once, and he was just letting things go. At the very least, she saw

Alberic's eyes close, and in that moment, he looked comfortable in his own skin. But what comfort was there in falling to your death, in abandoning what little life had to offer?

Wynne didn't understand. Time had a habit of making things so distant so quickly.

She flew down, and could almost touch his soles now; all she needed was his ankle to grab, and Alberic would be safe. But Wynne saw the ground coming closer fast. The thought of landing head-first into gravel stopped Wynne for a second, a second too long. Alberic was so close now that trying was impossible, but she couldn't look away.

Not when Alberic was glowing a bright orange. To Wynne, Alberic was like the Sun. No, not the muted white that was constantly hidden by the Veil. She was looking again at the bright, golden sun outside the Veil, where the outside world was. Alberic was ready.

* * *

Alberic wanted to scream. It wouldn't help accomplish anything, save for letting go of all the anger and disappointment he felt in his life, his village, his efforts, his friend Wynne, and himself. But if he could let those go, perhaps the burning feeling in his gut would go away. Alberic opened his mouth, and let out a weak gasp as a powerful gust of wind poured into his mouth. He couldn't quite see where the wind was coming from, nor what had caused it.

That wasn't going to stop him. If anything, Alberic deserved the right to scream for all that he had been dealt. It angered him that even nature wanted him to shut up, but no one, nothing was going to stop him. Alberic opened his mouth, and tried to scream again.

A deafening roar reverberated through his ears, and the world in front of Alberic lit up in amber. As soon as Alberic closed his mouth, the world returned to its dull gray color, save for little flickering tongues of orange flames on the trees.

Flames?

There were flames on the trees. But why would there be flames on them?

Alberic squeezed his eyes shut, and peeked down at his right arm. What he saw was not an arm covered in white ice, but now rollings hills of gray scales. The earth, cool and a bit damp to the touch, very easily collapsed and molded under his claws. When he lifted it, he could see triangular tips gouge into the loam.

Alberic closed his eyes, and breathed cold air into his lungs. Through his scale-tipped ears that were lined with stone-cold scales, lukewarm blood pulsed, throbbed, and rushed through arteries and veins; the quiet thrum of the flow was all he could hear, aside from the distant echoes of the wind carried from far beyond.

He followed those echoes. The trees felt like twigs to him; they simply snapped as he shoved trunks, brambles, and branches aside. Each thud of the step was a thud in his heart, for Alberic could feel himself warm up as the sky became brighter and brighter. Alberic began to pull himself forward, and soon he had erupted into a gallop through the forest. Trees fell under his weight as his legs pushed hard against the floor, and for a moment, Alberic's vision was covered in brilliant gold. It didn't last for so long, though; after the brief moment to relish in the very tangible, the very real sunlight, Alberic sunk into the cold, miserable gray once again.

He wanted to… no, *needed* to feel that sunlight on his face. It felt too good to be real, but all it took was a leap. So Alberic broke into a sprint again, and jumped. This time, he spread his body wide, just to make sure that every inch of himself could feel what he had felt before.

And Alberic could see it again: the golden sun, the crowns of white upon a rolling field of mist, the blue sky. Alberic could feel himself falling again, but he was falling too soon. So he extended an arm towards the sky, and his limbs began to flail uselessly.

Well, except for a pair. Something along Alberic's shoulders spread wide and flexed. With a great push, Alberic's head lurched down as his body pulled itself higher and higher through the air. It didn't take very long to feel the burn of working limbs that he never worked before, but the sun was still calling for him. Alberic flapped his wings, and flew higher.

The mist, once an imposing wall that threatened to swallow everything, shrank into something like a soft blanket. A soft, cool breeze rushed past Alberic's face, but as his wings flattened, Alberic was taken higher and higher by a tepid updraft. The white continued to shrink away from him, and soon enough, Alberic saw a brilliant band of green on the horizon. From this distance, it was too far away to tell whether it held grasslands, a forest, a town, or even one of those vast, imposing cities described only in stories. Not that any one of those made much of a difference.

Dragons, like and unlike Alberic, were out there on the horizon.

If he could defeat his own, those dragons too could be defeated.

# THE FROG WHO WATCHES

## By Colleen Nguyen

In the start,
A frog sits on a lily pad,
On top of a lake ever so blue,
Under a sky so clear.
In a forest dense with trees
And lively with animals,
The frog sat on a lily pad,
In his beginning years.

As time moves on,
The frog sits on a lily pad,
On top of a lake slightly green,
Under a sky of gray.
In a forest with smaller groups of trees
And a quieter atmosphere,
The frog sat on a lily pad,
In his middle years.

Near his end,
The frog sits on a lily pad,
On top of a blue water fountain,
Under a sky no longer blue.
In a city filled with buildings
And the noises of cars,
The frog sat on a lily pad,
Watching the world change.

# FAULTY EXPECTATIONS ABOUT ANGELS

## By Monica Van

Angel with tattoos, piercings, blue hair,
Are you truly an Angel,
Or did I err?

Where is your tunic?
Where are your wings?
Have you fallen from Heaven,
From the throne of kings?

To us humans,
You look more Demon than Angel;
In your case, holiness seems estranged.

In your defense--
As if you were a criminal--
Who are we humans to judge you?
You have always looked so,
With your tattoos as birthmarks
And with your hair that blue.

Faulty expectations
Can never define any being,
Whether human or Angel;
Reality is a different shade
In appearance altogether.

You are an Angel,
And you know better than we
Humans, who, unholy in nature,
Will never be free
From our own
Expectations.

# My Youth

## By Emily Dang

I'm getting older by the minute. Time is slipping through my fingertips.
I'm holding on to something as dense as air,
I'm holding on to the false belief that maybe I won't grow up.
My eyes divert across the grid, I judge every pore of my skin.
My once pale complexion, tainted by the summer sun,
My silky, long hair, now chopped and butchered into split ends,
There are bags under my eyes. Wrinkles splattered on my face.
Faded scars and blemishes,
Every imperfection carries its own individual story,
Yet this chubby, childlike figure is thinning out for a matured frame,
The body of a powerful woman.
No doubt, I'm growing older.
A new chapter begins and it's time to turn the page.
New scars, new blemishes, new image.
Am I ready for this?
No. I don't think I'll ever be.
But time is endless and life will move on regardless.
Everyone, including you and me, grows up.

My youth is gone.

# ESCAPE

## By Kimberly Nguyen

"YOU'LL NEVER GET ME to tell you where the jewels are." Arabella twisted her body, the frayed rope scraped against her wrists before digging themselves into the back of her hands.

James's thin lips curved upward into a smirk. "In time, Arabella. In time."

Arabella shifted in her seat, the muscles in her body tightening at the sound of her name on his lips. James stood with his back facing her. He slid the remnants of an old picture, yellowed around its worn, uneven edges into their proper place on the steel tabletop. The grooves of the pieces interlocked as they formed the image of a young woman with her arms draped around a little girl's shoulders. Both had grins spread across their faces.

A single light bulb hung from the ceiling, casting its dim light onto James's back. Arabella scanned his frame, her eyes resting on the small of his back where the outline of a gun protruded from under his steel blue t-shirt.

"You don't scare me, you know," Arabella said. "I won't tell you where they are."

James turned his head, his eyes darting over his shoulder at Arabella. She was still where he had left her, seated on a small wooden chair, her raven hair draped over her shoulders to the waist of her red laced dress.

"Just tell me where the jewels are." James whipped around and lunged at Arabella, his face stopping just inches from hers. "And I promise no one will get hurt."

Eyebrows furrowed, lips pulled tight into a straight line, Arabella stared into the forest green eyes that lie before her. They flashed a look of recognition before clouding over with hatred and contempt.

"What happened to you?" she asked. "You were my best friend."

James stepped back, the shadows from the light bulb resting on the bridge of his nose and his cheekbones, highlighting his features. His face was a blank slate, hidden from all emotion except for his eyes. Deep green eyes, half hidden by heavy eyelids, draped in long dark lashes, that flashed pain and sadness.

"James, look at me. What you're doing, this, it isn't going to change anything." Arabella's voice softened. "They're gone."

James's eyes darted to the ground. "It's late, we'll continue this tomorrow." He turned and walked to the other end of the room where a makeshift wooden staircase led out of the basement. "You should get some sleep." The steps creaked in protest as he climbed them.

"It doesn't matter how long you keep me here, you know." Arabella craned her neck to look at James. "There's no point." She leaned back against the chair, listening to him leave through the door at the top of the steps.

The room was plunged into silence, except for the soft buzz of the light bulb that hung in the center of the room. Arabella's eyes darted from wall to wall, then back at the staircase. *I need to get out of here...I've been away for too long.*

Arabella twisted her shoulders as she pulled at her restraints. The ropes clawed at her raw skin. Her eyes closed and she bit her lip as her left hand slid further out of her restraints. With her feet planted firmly on the ground, Arabella pushed against the back of the chair and put all her weight into pulling her left hand from the ropes.

With her hands free, Arabella pulled herself onto her feet. She scanned the room for an exit. To her right, the wooden staircase laid half hidden by shadows. *He'd hear me coming up the stairs.* Her eyes scanned the room again; they fell on the window that sat on the concrete wall behind her. White moonlight streamed in through the layer of dust that coated the glass.

Pushing the chair under the window, Arabella hoisted herself onto the seat. The chair wobbled on its uneven legs. She grabbed the window sill to balance herself. Her fingers ran across the dusty sill until she found a latch. Reaching with both her hands, she felt for the lock and opened it. The window swung open as a rush of cold air shot through the opening, sending her hair into her face. Arabella cursed under her breath as she glanced back at the staircase. She reached her arms out the window and felt the soft grass outside. The sheet of dew that had settled on the ground stuck to her skin as Arabella dragged herself out from the basement.

Her bare feet stumbled over rocks and broken branches but she did not stop. She moved through the rows of trees, the branches scraping against her legs and face, the night air stinging her skin, until the glowing lights of the city shone before her. Arabella fumbled down the streets, her body swaying from exhaustion. The only thing on her mind were her jewels.

She stopped before a small yellow house trimmed with white, its windowsills lined with flowerbeds of deep red roses. Her hand supported her weight on the wall beside her, Arabella reached down and pulled a single key from underneath a potted plant placed by the door. As she opened the door, a warm light flooded onto the porch and the familiar scent of lilac candles filled the air. Arabella slammed the door shut behind her, flopping her back against the door. She closed her eyes as the tightness in her chest dissolved, her breathing slowed, and her shoulders slumped back. *I made it.*

She forced herself to continue moving, and she staggered into the bedroom. Two bassinets filled the center of room, each draped in pink cotton sheets laced with white ruffles. Arabella tiptoed to the bassinets, peering in at the two baby girls asleep inside. She could see their little bellies steadily rise and fall from under the sheets.

"My little jewels." She reached down and with a single finger and brushed the short strands of dark hair from their foreheads. One of the babies squirmed at her touch. "My precious baby girls, there's nothing in this world I wouldn't give up for you." Arabella leaned in and kissed their foreheads.

The faint sound of keys rattled at the front door. Arabella jolted upward, she froze. *Please be my imagination.* The keys sounded again, this time as they opened the front door.

"Arabella, I know you're here. I saw you come in." James's voice came from the living room. Arabella peered around the the doorframe. She could see James's back at the end of the hallway, in his hands were her keys. Arabella cleared her throat, making her presence known as she walked into the hallway, closing the door behind her.

"James." She straightened her back and made herself as large as possible. "Get out of my house."

James turned around to face her. "I'm here for the girls...your precious little jewels," he mocked.

"How is this going to bring them back? Open your eyes James. Your wife, your daughter, they're gone. Replacing them with my girls isn't going to bring them back."

James's eyes rolled shut, his lips parting as he let out a soft sigh. "I already know that. They're dead." Tears welled in his eyes. "And it's all my fault." He threw his hands over his face, his shoulders heaving as sobs escaped his mouth.

Arabella walked toward James and placed a hand on his shoulder. "There was nothing you could do. If you had gone into that fire, we would have lost you too."

James jerked away from Arabella's hand. "I should have died with them."

"Stop it. Are you forgetting that I loved them too?" she shouted. "I can't lose my brother too, not like this." James slumped onto the ground, sobbing.

Arabella sat down beside him and wrapped her arms around his weeping mass. "It's my fault. I knew you were hurting but I was so busy grieving myself that I wasn't there for you. I was the one who let you get to this point...I can't believe I didn't see that coming."

58

# WAKING UP

## By Gabrielle Romero

On the weekends,
I expected to wake up
to you in the kitchen cooking
Like you always did

On my birthday,
I expected to wake up
to you singing happy birthday
Like you always did

That summer,
I expected to wake up
to the door closing as you left for church
Like you always did

In the middle of the night,
I expected to wake up
to your gentle hand saving me from a nightmare
Like you always did

On May 3rd, 2011,
I expected to wake up
and express all the gratitude I have for you
Like I always should have

That evening,
I expected you to wake up

# WHO YOU REALLY ARE

## By Mikayla Reilly

I see you standing there,
With your head held high
Your neatly pressed clothes
And your freshly polished shoes.

Your body oozes with confidence
While your eyes shine with fear.
No one notices your lies,
But I see the truth.

They'll pass you by
And believe you're all right,
Because you're the It Guy,
Who has everything right.

But they'll soon find out,
And everyone will see
Who you really are:
The fragile little boy.

No one understands
What your life is like.
The life they think you live
Is really just a lie.

The dirty little secrets you hide,
The ones you keep deep down inside
So no one knows who you really are.

I look into your cold, dark eyes
And see the little boy you trapped,

And I don't know why,
But I'll find out. I always do.

I will be there
To unmask
Who you really are.

# DEAD PEN

## By Becky Lee

Oh, dear pen,
Why must you run out of ink?
Your cartridge appears full,
And yet you won't write.
I try to warm you up
With my hands, with my breath,
And still, your black ink fails to spill.
You were my favorite pen--
My only black pen.
You wrote so nicely, so thinly, so finely.
But no. Your ink had to freeze,
And now, dear pen,
You can no longer write.

# The Phoenix

## By Daniel Bui

The sky is on fire.
Blood roses ignite the horizon, like brushes along a painting.
The crimson yellow dancers waltz along the clouds,
Casting a citrus gleam.
The sun embraces her children
Holding them closely in the breast of her lit forge,
She breathes out life for us all.
The red inferno that combusts the stars breathes out life for us all
Slowly, the evening ocean reaches from the west
The shores of night
And the impending death of this bright light,
For now, it blazes on and on, ever so valiantly against the starry waters
Like Freedom, holding her great flame over the raging sea
It will soon be swallowed in the mouth of darkness, the end of its flare
But it will return once again, lighting its brilliance and beauty over the world
It will return....

But how can I be certain? The truth is, nobody can.
For such, the beauty of life is not everlasting.
This life, this life, how brilliantly it flashes
A blessing so valuable and divine, it can be swept away in the currents.
If it be from a terrible burning lash that engulfs us, or the prophecy of old
Or a meteor, lo and behold, sending us into the giant hearth in the sky
How easy it is to breathe in life....how much easier it is to draw our last breath
This blessing from the stars that we have been given, so many of us take it for
granted.
We cannot dwell on our gifts, not even for a second, or we drown.
This life, yes this life, it is not everlasting.
Cease from dousing the flames within you, let it shine for Gaia to witness,
Kindle the trails, burn the films, soar the waters,
For one day, it will no longer be yours.

# THE WOES OF JIMMY DOE

## By Maggie Tieu

BEHIND THE DOOR, A young man with dark rings around his eyes contrasting his pale face revealed himself.

"And I believe you are Mr…" The therapist scanned the clipboard in his hand. "…Jimmy Doe?"

"Yup, the one and only. Thank God I'm talking to you today, Doc." Jimmy beamed and made his way into the room. "Because if I went on for one more day, I might as well just lose my mind."

The therapist scribbled onto his clipboard and nodded once. "Is that so? Please do share." He motioned Jimmy towards the large couch in the center of the room.

Jimmy flopped down onto the puffy couch and kicked up his legs onto the small coffee table in front of him, knocking off an antique vase . The therapist dived over the coffee table and clutched the vase to his chest before it hit the ground. He landed with a muffled thud.

"Now, I just wanna be upfront," Jimmy said. "I do want to get help, but I'm just no good in a conversation--let alone speak about my issues and whatnot. You know what I'm saying?"

The therapist gasped. "I-is that so?" He set the vase back onto the center of the coffee table. "Do you need me to list some of the other methods that are available for this session?"

Jimmy leaned onto the couch arm and knitted his brows together, staring at the wooden floor.

"Don't worry Mr. Doe, I would be more than happy to--"

"Wait, Doc, I got it." Jimmy jumped from his seat. "I know how to do this now." Jimmy stood on top of the couch cushions and tapped away on his phone.

The therapist stared at him with wide eyes before uttering, "W-well that's wonderful, Mr. Doe. Would you mind taking a seat and share wha-"

"Why didn't I realize it sooner? I'm not a man of speech but a man of music! If Linkin Park can sing nonsense about its inner feelings, then so can I." The room turned dark. A spotlight shined down on Jimmy.

The therapist jumped off his seat and turned in all directions around the room, panting. "What in tarnation-"

Jimmy stepped onto the small coffee table with a thunderous stomp, making the vase topple off the table.

"Good gracious, no!" The therapist shrieked as he leaped once again over the table.

By the time the therapist sat himself up on the ground with the vase in hand, a small group of people appeared out from nowhere and gathered together holding various instruments connected to speakers that touched the ceiling. Jimmy stood there in the spotlight and raised a wireless microphone to his mouth.

"I may not be a conversationalist in the brain, Doc, but I am a *singer* by the heart.

*'One day under the bright light*
*I open my eyes to find myself sleeping on the kitchen floor*
*I say to myself, this isn't my room*
*Then my roommates tell me I've been*
*SLEEP-WALKING AGAIN*
*SLEEP-WALKING AGAIN*
*HIT IT BOYS-"*

Before the guitarist could hit a chord on the electric guitar, the therapist unplugged the stereo and instruments. The group of people groaned as the therapist pushed them out. The door shut. The therapist smacked his forehead onto the door frame, appreciating the new silence in the room.

The therapist turned to Jimmy. "Alright Mr. Doe, you have an issue with sleepwalking. That alone would've sufficed."

"Oh...Well, it didn't feel right without a sick beat, you know? It would've had more gusto and passion with some background music and special light effects--"

"Please take a seat, Mr. Doe".

"Alright," Jimmy muttered, taking a seat on the couch.

The therapist slumped his shoulders and gave a huff of relief. He set the vase on his alcohol counter in the corner of the office then pulled up a chair in front of Jimmy. "So from your earlier...performance, you mentioned that your roommates caught you sleepwalking on multiple occasions?"

"Yup, I woke up on the kitchen floor every time. I've tried all kinds of things to try to get rid of it." Jimmy leaned back on the couch and smiled to himself. "Like staying up twenty-four-seven with nothing but coffee and ice water, marathoning all the episodes of *Lost*. But now I just have a pile of receipts from Starbucks, a possible caffeine tolerance, and a memorized script of Naveen Andrews lines from season one."

The therapist scribbled onto his clipboard. "Has anything else occurred that seemed peculiar?"

Jimmy stared at the therapist in silence. "Everytime I wake up, I hear these faint voices calling out my name."

"Voices you say? Sounds perplexing, Mr. Doe."

"No Doc, you gotta understand. These voices are faint, but if you really try to listen to them, are actually quite beautiful. It's like listening to the soundtrack from *Wicked* or hearing Morgan Freeman's voice." Jimmy gazed up at the ceiling with dreamy eyes with his hands over his chest. "Or even like listening to a choir of angels from the highest tier of heaven."

It was then that birds barged through the office door and swarmed around the room. The swarm of birds formed a hurricane of angry, constant tweeting and sharp feathers yanked around by the violent windstorm. They swallowed both Jimmy and the therapist in the hurricane of feathery hell.

"What's happening now? Jimmy Doe, what is the meaning of this?" The therapist screeched in horror. Sweat dripped from his forehead.

"I-I don't know, Doc. I think God is finally coming to get me for watching a really terrible show. Doc, I'm scared, I didn't mean to watch all the seasons of *Lost*."

"Mr. Doe, this isn't the time to be--"

"It's just...it's just that I saw Naveen Andrews was in it, and he's just so *handsome*." Jimmy screamed and buried his face into the therapist's damp sweater.

As Jimmy's tears mixed with the sweat in the therapist's soaking sweater, the hurricane of hell dimmed down. At the end of the office, a glowing figure stood in the doorway. The glowing figure stepped away from the light and approached the trembling duo. Jimmy gasped at the figure before him. Silent and sweating, the therapist shoved Jimmy toward the glowing figure. Jimmy stumbled onto his knees. He looked up and whispered, "Naveen Andrews, is that you? Did you die already?"

The figure placed a firm hand on Jimmy's shoulder and chuckled, "No, I am but an angel sent from the heavens."

"What-- why are you here?" The therapist croaked.

"Don't be afraid, sweaty one, for I was sent here by God to say that this young man has something special." The angel patted Jimmy on the shoulder. "I came down here to tell you that your voice alone has touched the heavens."

The therapist, hidden behind his couch, threw up his arms. "You've got to be kidding me. My office was trashed because of that?"

The room turned dark, and a spotlight shined on the angel and Jimmy.

"No," the therapist yelled. Several angels descended into the office, while Jeff Buckley's *Hallelujah* played in the background.

Tears dripped down Jimmy's face. "You mean it, holy angel?"

"I do Jimmy. You've been chosen by God for quite some time now, actually. Although we angels had issues trying to get you to wake up during the night." The angel shrugged. "That's why you've been waking up in the kitchen. It's hard to fit a band of angels in a tiny apartment."

"Oh, so you don't wreck his place but wrecked mine?" The therapist stomped across the room to turn the lights back on. "Where's the liberty and justice in that--what kind of government do you even have in heaven? This is all just unfair."

"No need for that nonsense. Please holy angel, take me to where I belong." Jimmy offered both hands to the angel.

The angel gave Jimmy a gentle smile and snapped her fingers. Jimmy sprouted wings from his back. The background music grew louder and louder, drowning the angels' cheers. In the commotion, the therapist made his way toward the alcohol counter and poured himself a shot of whiskey. After a long sip, the therapist spit out his drink when Jimmy and the angel burst through the ceiling, leaving a large crater. The group of singing angels and the flock of birds spiraled out of the room through the crater in a flurry of feathers and bright, flashing light.

After what it seemed like hours, the therapist peered around his feather-covered office and the kicked the rubble from the ceiling. He sighed in the silent room and slumped onto the floor with his back to counter. The vase toppled off of the counter and shattered onto the floor. The lonely therapist shed a single tear.

# No Longer

## By Katie Luong

With your rhymes and poems,
I didn't know the answer.
It makes me think,
Wondering what the hell did I do?
A past problem I hadn't seen before.

You rant and complain
about my misery,
but you seem to forget
That you were the cause.

Here we are,
up against an invisible barrier that stood in our way.
Abandoned, forgotten.
I gave up on life.

Day after day,
I welcome the demons held within.
No longer myself, I wanted everything to end,
Depression and anxiety became my best friends,
No longer able to hold the last strand of sanity.

I wanted this pain to end,
It was long overdue.
My hands held a trusted old friend,
Capable of ending all my misery.
In a single blow, I no longer felt pain.
The day I was gone, and you were late.

You held me close,
You beg me not to leave you,
Alone in the dark and lonely world.

But it's too late.
You pushed me away.

Alone in this world, you realized that
Going around the globe, you changed lives.
You see them frown
scrapes visible for others to see.
You told them they were beautiful, they were perfect.

They don't need to change for one person.
Be themselves, be you.
One experience changed a person.
That person will change millions.

No longer sad. No longer regretting.
You were glad, you changed many.

# TO ME

## By Daniel Bui

Here's to someone I know,
The one who led me through and through
The one who I can call the world's greatest lover.
With the smile of a sun, I don't take cover
She taught me many things
Which I haven't forgotten up 'til today.
To me, she's an angel
She's Michael, Uriel, Raphael
She gave me the strength to look up,
She gave me the love to move forward,
She gave me a lot of things, this I know.

....We all have weaknesses, the sad story of life
In such a big world, she finds herself lost
To me, she is the world.
I want to be her tour guide
In such a giant ocean, she's lost at sea
To me, she's a mermaid
I want to be her sailor
I want her to know, I'll always be there
I'm with you, all the way
Every step you take, I'll be by you
Everything that I do, I do for you
In the name of love, we shall conquer any beasts in our way
In the name of love, we'll swim muddy waters, scale rocky cliffs
We're in this together, and I'll never give up on us
To me, we are meant to be.
I love you, so love yourself
Together we will live, love, laugh
Yes we're in this together
You and me, we'll look at what the world has for us to see.

# GLASS

## By Gabrielle Romero

Your legs are not yet strong enough
to walk on your own,
Your mind is not yet developed enough
to know where your steps will lead you,
Your skin is not yet thick enough
to withstand the harsh road,
You are not yet old enough
to handle the broken glass coming your way.
So your tiny hands grasp my fingers,
and your feet rest on mine.
while I willingly take on the road for you,
While I walk on glass so you don't have to.

# PUPPY LOVE
## By Lily Do

WHEN A TEENAGER TURNS fifteen, they expect to learn how to drive and probably want to start planning their sixteenth birthday. Who knew that when I became fifteen, I would be helping my family pay the bills. I didn't expect my dad to come into my small room. I didn't expect him to sit down on my navy blue sheets while he pushed aside my homework and twiddled with his thumbs. I didn't expect it when his voice shook and his eyes glossed over while he told me he was going to visit my mom.

My mom had a stroke exactly nine months, two weeks, six days, and ten hours from the moment my dad walked into my room. She was currently at the local hospital a couple streets down : Orange Coast Memorial Medical Center, Room 212 on the second floor. She went back recently for a checkup, but the doctors told her to stay overnight for a couple days to run a few more tests. I didn't think anything of it, but my dad had been stressing over this matter to the point where he called in sick yesterday to be with my mom.

I could still remember the day of her stroke. It was on the same day of a big biology test that was going to determine whether or not I would be able to maintain my 4.2 GPA. I studied all night before and even asked my dad to quiz me on my vocabulary words at the dining table. We ate dinner afterward with my little brother, Zander, of soft tofu stew my mom made. It was Friday when I took the test during second period. I was on question twenty three when a ring disrupted our quiet cell of a classroom. My teacher groaned and walked across the room to pick up the phone. All I remember next was being called to the office because my dad was there to pick me up due to a family emergency. My parents weren't that close to their brothers and sisters, so I didn't understand why I had to leave my test behind until I sat down in our car and I asked him what happened.

That day, my dad took me back from my haunting memories and called out to me. "The doctor called in. Something came up, so I need to go see how she is doing. Make sure you get to school tomorrow with your brother and pick him up. I left some money on the counter and I'm going to call in to work to see if I can get a substitute to come in," my dad explained.

My dad sat sideways, allowing me to examine his profile. He slouched forward and clenched his hands between his legs. He had aged so much within these past months ever since my mom had the stroke. I was only fourteen at the time, freshly thrown into high school while my younger brother, Zander, who was ten, faced problems of his own. Both my parents were pretty young for having two children. My dad was only in his mid-thirties and worked as a teacher at Sunny Hills High School, teaching Korean as a foreign language. He was always carefree and was the more relaxed parent. Then, there is my dear mother. She was only thirty-two when the incident occurred. It was a complete shock because my parents were extremely healthy. They always forced me to drink all my milk and to eat all my vegetables, yet it was expected. My dad said it was because she had high blood pressure from the stress she had from working too much. She was a tutor at the Huntington Beach Library, but I didn't understand why she was so stressed over it. There were plenty of workers and a constant amount of students coming for help every day. I just didn't understand.

Ever since that dreadful day, my family has never been the same. We were never that close before, but now we spent all our time together, understanding that time was precious. My dad brought work home and spent less time at school so that he could take care of my mom. My mom spent less days at the library because there was always something else that made her feel ill. I got ten times closer to my brother and have been there for him ever since; I always took him out when we needed breaks and explained to him what our family was going through.

I didn't know that the bills were becoming a strain on my family, especially on my dad, so when he came into my room and asked me to help him out, I knew I had to get a job the next day.

The library was the easiest way to do that. I always spent my time there with my brother to study or volunteer since my mom worked there. I was able to sign up to become a tutor like her and worked on Mondays, Wednesdays, and Fridays. These past couple of months, I worked and gave most of my money to my dad. Now, as a fifteen-year-old, I really don't mind as much. I had been saving up for a car, and it's nice having some extra money laying around. I get to spoil my brother because I know my parents don't have time to look out for him anymore.

Working wasn't too bad. I got to tutor kids from a wide variety of ages and volunteered whenever I could. The plain routine became boring until one day I got a call while working the reception desk. "Welcome to the Huntington Beach Library. How may I help you?" I said into the phone.

"Hello. Could put a book on hold for me?" a male voice spoke. His voice was quiet and velvety.

It took me off guard because it sounded so youthful compared to the calls I usually got: calls from the elderly asking about on various library events. I cleared my throat. "Yes, of course. What's the title, author, and your name?"

"Romeo and Juliet by William Shakespeare. My name is William Pierce."

I punched the information into the computer to make sure we still had it and placed his book on hold. "Okay, you're all set. Just come by the desk to pick it up."

We traded pleasantries and I hung up. Now came the hard part: locating the book in the vast library.

* * *

People always say that time is running out. It truly is. How could an individual do so many things in such little time? You could spend the time going on a wide adventure, following old mythical maps to find buried treasure or maybe even taking out the time to develop your relationship with a significant other and fall in love. Maybe even sail the seven seas and travel to another planet. There are just too many books to read in such a short amount of time. Yet it surprised me that a special someone with such a smooth voice wanted to read such an old play. I understood that the story of love at first sight paired with beautifully woven language can capture anyone's heart with millions of copies sold, but there were so many newer and more contemporary pieces of art to discover.

I travelled back to the front desk with a copy of Romeo and Juliet clenched in my hand and placed the book on the cart behind the desk and took a seat on the old wooden stool placed in front of the computer. While I checked up on the library's website for any unanswered emails, a familiar voice startled me.

"I'm here to pick up a book."

I looked forward to find a chest covered by a simple black hoodie. My eyes wandered up to his face. With chestnut brown hair tossed haphazardly on top of his head and his black glasses slightly askew, he looked as if he had just rolled out of bed. Literally. I barely got a glimpse of his blue eyes before they took interest in the dirty carpeted floor. He coughed under my gaze and shifted his weight from one foot to the other.

"Oh, sorry, hello! What's your name?" I said with a smile. Customer service was key to an efficient library.

"William--"

"--Pierce. Looking for Romeo and Juliet right?" I interrupted. William nodded, but he still didn't meet my gaze. It was nice to finally put a voice to a face. William looked around my age, probably in high school, but his chubby cheeks and round face gave him the face of a puppy. I just wanted to reach over the table to pinch his now rosy cheeks. I turned around to grab the book on the cart behind me and placed it in front of him. As I stood up, I realized I was barely coming up to his shoulders.

He rummaged in his back pocket to pull out his library card while I continued to stare at him openly. He was just too adorable to look away from.

"Thank you. Have a nice day, William," I said, sliding his book towards him.

He smiled. "Have a good one, Zoella." He walked away toward the maze of bookshelves.

I sat back down on the stool in shock. How did he know my name? He never even looked up to meet my gaze. He couldn't have gone to my school either because I would have recognized a face like that.

Well, maybe volunteering at the library was about to get better this year.

# 5

## By Lily Do

These five things make me
feel alive. Yet I must
live among those who can't
taste the pounding bass or
smell the memorizing, dancing lights.

It doesn't matter the place.
Surrounded by sand and bodies,
or cruising a deserted highway.
I can savor the noises
one measure at a time.

It doesn't matter the time,
From the alarm clock ringing,
To the stars saying goodnight,
I can visualize the vibrations
And touch the delicate notes.

Hearing is the ultimate sense.
Listening to the unison of
melodic voices and flowing lyrics.
Tempo rising and falling to
where you can't keep track.

Listening to my heart beat
faster and faster until I
can't taste, smell, feel, or touch.
Only hearing the last beat
of my favorite song end.

# MY MISFORTUNE

## By Leianna Giryan

Tragedy always falls upon me.
Even today, the day of such a storm,
Drops of water fall from my clothes,
My boots are filled,
I am soaked.

Standing there in the doorway,
I plaster the largest frown on my face.
What are the odds that my umbrella would break?
No winds were present and yet,
I am soaked.

Drag my feet across the tiles,
A trail of mud leaks,
My love sees me, slouching forward.
He comes to take my clothes
And comforts me,
Wrapping his arms around my shoulders.
I no longer believe anything good happens.
He hushes my cries and
Dries my wet eyes.
I cry not because I am soaked
But because I always have misfortune.
So I stand there bare,
Cold beneath, cold of my skin,
Sobbing to him.
I am saddened, but he,
Like everyone, else does not understand
My misfortune.

# LIAR

## By Katia Navarrete


January 1, 2009, 00:05

*I know.*

I know you are currently looking at this *damned* journal, Mother.

*I know.*

January 2, 2009, 18:23

I know. I know. I know. I know. I know. I know. *I know.*

January 3, 2009, 14:56

She gave me a lecture of what I have written here.

I wasn't listening half the time she was talking.

I've noticed her mind was elsewhere,

As if she had something better to do.

*As if I didn't matter.*


I didn't understand why she gave me this journal on New Year's.


I didn't understand why she wanted to *help* me.

*I didn't understand why.*

January 4, 2009, 16:21

I was walking home from school until I saw a rundown car in the driveway.

*I already knew what was going to happen.*

The driver was honking repeatedly while women sang in the backseat.

*I already knew what was going to happen.*

I saw her speed walk in her heels toward the car.

*I already knew what was going to happen.*

They all cheered when they saw her in a dress she bought.

*I already knew what was going to happen.*

She hopped in the passenger seat with a slam of the door.

*I already knew what was going to happen.*

The piece of trash reversed with screeching wheels and sped off.

*I already knew what was going to happen.*

She left to go drinking with her friends.
A new record.
Four days to get back how things used to be.
*I guess that was her New Year's resolution.*

January 5, 2009, 20:19

She didn't come home last night.
She didn't come home last night.
*She didn't come home last night.*

January 6, 2009, 19:02

I didn't bother going to school today.
I'm worried sick about her.
She wasn't answering my calls.
She *must* have been at her friend's house.
She *must* have her phone turned off.


That's why she didn't answer me.
*That's why she didn't answer me.*
This wasn't the first time she was missing,
I'm worrying about nothing.
She's going to come back.
*She always does.*

January 7, 2009, 14:45

I went to one of her friend's house, one of the last places I haven't been.
*She lied.*
A woman in her late thirties told me my mother got dropped off at my house.
*She lied.*
The smirk on her face didn't convince me.
*She lied.*

January 8, 2009, 10:16

I looked for her in local bars and motels.
*She wasn't there.*

January 9, 2009, 21:51

She was in an alley with a rope wrapped around her bicep.
*I've found her.*
Her favourite dress was ripped to shreds.
*I've found her.*
Her heels were nowhere to be found.
*But I've found her.*

I couldn't bear the pang in my chest.
Her left cheek. Her eye. Her lip. Her neck. Her stomach. Her thighs.
She's a complete lunatic, but she gave birth to me. That was *enough* for me.
She tried to help herself for my sake, that was *enough* for me.
She tried to save herself and me, that was *enough* for me.
That was *enough* for me to wrap my jacket around her.
For me to pick up her petite figure.
For me to take her back home.
*That was enough for me to love my mother again.*

January 10, 2009, 13:32

*I don't understand.*

January 11, 2009, 22:43

I don't know what has gotten into to her yesterday.
When I took her back home, she was covered in *scum*.
I wanted to bathe her, but I didn't want to wake her up.
*It's been awhile since I've seen my mother so peaceful.*
Her long lashes against her naturally rosy cheeks.
*It's been awhile since I've seen my mother so peaceful.*
Her freckles sprinkled on her nose and cheeks.
*It's been awhile since I've seen my mother so peaceful.*
Her bleached short hair surrounded her oval face.
*It's been awhile since I've seen my mother so peaceful.*
The wrinkles I had always teased her about were barely visible.
*It's been awhile since I've seen my mother so peaceful.*

If you looked past her bruised face and body, you'd wonder if she were an angel from the heavens.
If you looked past her bruised face and body, you'd wonder if she smiled twenty-four seven.
If you looked past her bruised face and body, you'd wonder if she spread happiness and told corny jokes.

When I snapped out of my thoughts, I carefully cleaned her wounds.
I froze when she groaned in pain.
I didn't want to wake her up into the monster that raised me.
*It was selfish of me.*
I didn't care at the moment.
After I finished, I dressed her into some pajamas I found in her closet.
I adored my mother's beauty for what seemed like hours on end.

*She didn't need the makeup.*

I kept myself busy cleaning around the house that night.
I searched for her *medications* and cigarettes in every possible place.
I hid them in my room.
I poured liquor down the drain, not caring if my mother got upset with me.
I swept the carpet.
I washed the pile of dishes in the sink.
I scrubbed the carpet.
I cleaned the wretched bathroom.

I checked on her every hour, worried if something might happen to her.
I thanked the stars for keeping her asleep and safe.
I took a chair and placed it beside her bed.
As much as I tried to stay up, I fell into the *hellish* slumbers.

She woke me up yesterday, screaming profanities in my face.
My body was killing me from sleeping on the plastic chair.
It had been a couple hours since I had passed out.
She kept yelling about her appointment.
I told her she had it days ago, on the day she went partying.
She shouted that it was yesterday, the fourth.
*That was when she snapped.*

She grabbed my hair and dragged me to her calendar on her *filthy* wall.
She dropped her grip when she noticed cigarette burns on the calendar.
She had a habit of burning them out on the days that have passed.
She left the room without a word.
I ran to my room, grabbing the bag of *medications* and jumping out the window.
She screeched when she saw her precious bottles empty.
*I was gone by then.*
I slept over at an old friend's house, sold him the *medications*.

We both knew he was my *only* option.
We both knew I was starting to crack.
He knows I'm starting not to care.
I know I'm turning into her.
I promised him I was going to be strong
I promised him I wouldn't cave into my old ways.

*I lied.*

I drank my heart out.
He helped me drink to my heart's content.
The stars disapproved of my decision.
The heavens counted my sins with every swallow.

I drank away my sorrows, my regrets, my guilt.
He distracted me from the pain.
The stars began to hide behind the gray clouds I've created.
The heavens shut the gate destined for me with a quiet click.
He led me to a dangerous path.

The path I promised myself I would never again go in.
The path my mother took.
The path that ruined our lives.
*She would have been proud.*

I noticed my mother at the place she met my father.
She hasn't been to that place since his *toxic* death.
When she noticed my gaze, I felt guilty.
When she noticed my drink in my hand, I felt guilty.
When she noticed my *friend*, I felt the need to confront her.
My *friend* nudged me when my attention wasn't on him.

I felt my mother's eyes burned with disappointment.
*She wasn't supposed to be there.*
He looked to where my attention was focused,
I felt his pride and righteousness radiate off himself.
*She wasn't supposed to be there.*
There were too many emotions coursing throughout my body.
*She wasn't supposed to be there.*
His hand clenched my forearm, he didn't want me to go.
*She wasn't supposed to be there.*

I didn't understand why she was there.
She never spoke to me, she just stared at me with disappointment.
*She never spoke to me, she just stared at me with disappointment.*

She's gone.
She's gone.
*She's gone.*

January 15, 2009, 22:12

I looked for her in local bars and motels.
*She wasn't there.*

January 16, 2009, 12:05

It's become a habit to look for her.
*I searched for her everywhere.*
I've always found her in all the wrong places.

I didn't know where to look anymore.
*I searched for her everywhere.*

January 17, 2009, 19:45

I refuse to go to the police for help.

*They'll take her away from me.*

I didn't know who to turn to.
*I didn't trust anyone.*
Not him.
*I didn't trust anyone.*
Not him.
*I didn't trust anyone.*

I was scared that something might happen to her.
I was worried what they would do if they found her.
*They'll take her away from me.*

January 18, 2009, 16:24

There was a missing person report on the news.
*I wasn't the one who called.*

January 19, 2009, 23:56

*What do I do?*

January 20, 2009, 00:00

*I didn't do anything, I swear.*
People gave me stares and glances.
*I didn't do anything, I swear.*
As if I'd done something wrong.
*I didn't do anything wrong, I swear.*

I went to visit her grave, it was full of white roses.
*I didn't put them there.*
Her grave was full of pictures of her and her friends, pictures of the past.
*I didn't put them there.*
Her grave was made out of the finest marble.
*I didn't have that money.*
Her engraving didn't make sense.

*In Loving Memory*
*Anastasia Lizbeth Hesnith*
*April 21, 1975- January 20, 2005*

It was wrong.
*It was all wrong.*

I went back home.
*Everything was a mess again.*
The stains reappeared, the pile of dishes reappeared.
*Everything was a mess again.*

I sat on the couch when I found a letter.
It made a crippling sound from under pillows of the couch.
It had my mother's handwriting scribbled on the stained yellow paper.
She hurt me.
*She left me.*
What could I do without her?
*She left me.*
Why did she leave me?
The letter was written in the year of her tombstone.

May 20, 2005, 00:00

# THE BLARING GUILT TRIP

## By Huan Dao

Let the moonlight and the sunset decide
If the needy really need them.
The concerned looks on their faces
Oh, I wish they were real.
To whomever it may concern,
The one who needs to change will never change,
But the one who doesn't does it every second.
Let the obnoxious scream
And let trails of the remains
Roam your ears.
Are you happy now?
And maybe your eyes will super glue themselves
To shut out the blaring guilt trip.
I hope you're satisfied.
The old footsteps will disappear in the blizzard
For the newer ones to come
But the guilt trip sure
Won't be so obvious.
Because tears don't blaze its trail,
And the desperation to live
Will eventually seep through
The layers and layers of your cold, dead heart.

# THE CHILD'S BURDEN

### By Jayson Mitchell

A shining sun-
kids running around, playing all day.
The warm rays are soothing;
gently landing on the bare skin.
No one cares, and all are free-
They lay in the soft reflective grass.

The kids are suddenly teens,
What happened to their gentle youth?
The sun never fading-
The kids are enjoying what time they have left.
Some have left and got jobs,
Others still linger and bask in the sun.

No matter what would happen-
They were always in that park.
Well-colored from the years of sun,
The kids, now adults, all begin to leave.

Taking a final look-
They leave the park at last.
A bittersweet departure,
But one day they will return.

Their kids will enjoy the sun-
Their kids will carry on their legacy.
These kids will be all that is left,
It is these kids that will follow in their parents' steps.
They too grow up every day in this solemn park--
They too grow dark from years in the sun.
Like their parents before them,
They take their children here.

Those children have a responsibility--
The decision whether to do something new--
Or do as they've always done--
Much like their parents and their parents before them.

# VERY DONE

## By Angela Chhun

Dark and merciless,
Mother nature stands.
Layers of cloth unfold,
Worn-out,
Torn umbrella in his hand

He sighs
Done with everything,
Destroyed.

Emptiness
Fills his sky
No clouds, no sunlight.

He returns home,
Warm and content.
A tired
Noiseless sleep,
He dozes off into eternity.

# INDIFFERENCE
## By Angelina Ngo

I swore to myself
That you'd never go a day without smiling.
At least, not when I was around.
I can't remember a time when my heart wasn't racing whenever you came by,
And I'd begin to hyperventilate.

How can I hide and deny my feelings for you,
when every time you pass by,
I fall deeper and deeper into that abyss called 'love.'
I was a fool to fall for you,

Though I hate to admit,
You're someone I can't have but want so damn bad
I fell in love with the sound of your voice,
The way your eyes would twinkle when you smiled,
Your insanely cute laughter that was like a sweet melody.

You ignited a burnt out flame from within.
The sparks would keep growing every time you glanced over,
when we accidentally made eye contact,
You were like a drug, and I was beyond addicted.

But I knew
The consequences, the risks, the concerns--
I knew it all.
I knew I would be the one left in endless tears,
the one left broken hearted,
the one left behind,

But even though it was pure agony, I would do it all over again.
Just so I could feel loved and cared for once more.

# CHILDHOOD FRIENDS
## By Joseph Ho

THE ALARM CLOCK BLARED on the wooden nightstand by the bed. Unfazed, Darrison rolled over on the bed with a groan, pulling the blue comforter over himself.

"Darrison, are you still home?" his mother called from downstairs. She swung open the door of his room. "Darrison, you're late for school."

Darrison twitched under the covers at his mother's voice and dragged himself up. He brushed through his hair with his fingers and looked at his mother. Dazed, he glanced around the room, unaware of what was going on. "Mom? What's wrong? Were you trying to cook breakfast again?" Darrison said with a grin.

"Very funny but no, not today darling." His mother rolled her eyes. "Hey Darrison, are you going to make it to school today?"

A rush of adrenaline burst through his veins. "I'm late." Darrison threw the covers off his body and jumped out of his bed.

The wind brushed past his hair and face. His books nearly flew out of his arms, and his backpack smacked against his back as he ran down the hall. When he entered his English classroom, everyone turned their heads and looked at him, including his teacher, Mrs. Cherry.

"Welcome back from the weekend, Darrison. You are a bit late but I'll Let it slide this time. We have a new student that just transferred to our school." Mrs. Cherry said, smiling. "So please introduce yourself to him."

Darrison stared around the class. When he spotted a boy with a shady black hood, he walked over to the empty seat next to him and sat down.

"Hi my name is Darrison. What's yours?" Darrison said.

The boy glanced at Darrison and turned away.

Mrs. Cherry's smile disappeared. "Now please take out your English textbooks and turn to page fifty."

Darrison stared over at the boy who glared at him from under his hood, crossed his legs, and turned away. Darrison considered offering to share his book with the new boy but figured his offer would be rejected so he turned to page fifty and read the Shakespearean chapter of *A Midnight's Summer Dream*. It wasn't long before Darrison's eyes began to droop and he fell asleep. He dreamt of his childhood--his best friend in preschool and how they were with each other all the time. Darrison forgot his name but he remembered the mournful look on his best friend's face when Darrison told him he was moving away.

"Darrison." Mrs. Cherry poked him with a ruler and tapped her foot.

"I-I'm alive... Shakespeare..." Darrison jolted up from his desk and picked up his book.

Mrs. Cherry sighed and looked at Darrison with disappointment. She released the class to leave and scolded Darrison. "Sleep early okay? You've been falling asleep constantly."

He nodded his head and asked, "Who's the new guy?"

"Oh? Are you talking about Adrian?" Mrs. Cherry asked. "He's still a little shy but with a little time he should open up more."

"He seems a bit...different, if you ask me. Anyways, I'll be on my way now." Darrison walked out of the class, waving a quick goodbye.

Walking in front of him was Adrian, the new student from his class. Darrison was heading to the snack bar but there something upsetting about the new boy. Adrian was knocking down the books of innocent students, bullying them. He shoved everyone who blocked his path and yelled at them for no reason. He was acting like he was dictator of the school. Darrison shook his head as he watched Adrian shove another classmate aside.

"What a jerk." Darrison mumbled under his breath.

"Move scrub." Adrian shoved Darrison aside to the wall. "Oops. My bad."

The sarcasm in his voice made Darrison so furious that his hatred for him grew. Instead of talking back, he wrapped his anger around his mind once more and dispersed it. *Don't get angry now Darrison...focus.*

Days passed by and at the end of the week, Mrs. Cherry had an announcement. She assigned partners for a class project. "And our last set of partners for the Shakespearean collaborative writing are you two." Mrs. Cherry pointed to Darrison and Adrian.

"What?" Darrison stood up immediately. "With him?"

"Yes, now sit back down," Mrs. Cherry said. "No exceptions."

Darrison shook his head in disbelief and looked over to Adrian. Adrian returned his stare.

"So, are we going to start planning how we're going to do this or what?" Adrian said.

Darrison nodded his head and they began planning everything. Adrian agreed to work at his own house and have Darrison come over. Darrison was going to bring over the writing.

"I guess I'll see you tomorrow, Saturday then," Darrison said.

91

Adrian stared at Darrison in silence and slid his sweatshirt hood on. Then he clicked on his phone and swiped the screen.

Darrison glanced over and saw a corgi wallpaper on Adrian's phone. He cupped his hands over his mouth to trap the tiny gasp from the corgi cuteness. It was too much for him. He had to look away at the bare wall on the left to calm himself; Darrison had a love for corgis and really wanted one, but his mother would never allow it. In the middle of his thoughts, the bell rang.

Saturday came quickly and Darrison stopped in front of a house with a front porch. Four white wooden pillars etched with golden patterns held up the roof of the porch. The exterior walls of the house were painted a light rose pink with a dash of white trim. A decorative street lamp stood next to the white arched front door of the house. The grass surrounding the house made it seem separated from the rest of the neighborhood, like a single house in the breeze on top of a mountain. Darrison was astonished by the exterior.

"Is this even his house?" His eyes widened. "It doesn't suit his personality."

The door creaked open and Adrian stepped outside. "Come on in."

When Darrison stepped inside, he heard a bark and paws scampering across the wooden floor. He turned around and a corgi jumped right on top of him.

"A corgi," Darrison said, shrieking with joy and excitement. "Oh my God."

"Let's go upstairs. This corgi will distract us," Adrian said. "I mean distract *you*."

When they reached his room, Darrison's eyes glistened at the beauty of the black walls and the shiny constellations on the ceiling. Then he was taken aback at the mess in the room. Clothing sprawled across the ground and trash everywhere.

"Don't mind the mess," Adrian said. "You're just here for work."

"Ah okay. Let's start working then." Darrison took out the writing supplies. The boys started the Shakespearean writing assignment.

"So, Adrian. Do we write about a comedy or a romance writing?" Darrison asked him.

Adrian stared at the writing for awhile then his eyes widened. "Want to play a game before we start? It'll only be a quick moment."

Darrison's face swirled in confusion. He was unsure if they should waste their time on a game but he agreed anyways.

Adrian explained the game carefully to Darrison. "One person has to draw a picture that they can explain and the opponent has to figure it out. That's it."

Darrison held the tip of his chin with his fingers. "Well, that does sound quick and fun."

"What? You don't like it?"

"No, I do like it. It's just…" Darrison turned away from Adrian. *Wasn't this game familiar? It was like he played it long time ago.* "I just had Déjà vu. That's all."

Adrian pulled out a thin white sheet of paper and a thick black marker. He gave it to Darrison and urged him to draw something that he could explain. Darrison looked down at the paper with a serious face.

"I think I'll try to draw this." Darrison's arm swirled in many ways and the thick lines formed houses, trees, the street, and a sign that said *Barcks Street.* Then he wrote the image's name on the back. "What is this drawing?"

"It's a neighborhood? Almost like the neighborhood I moved here from," Adrian said. "It even has the same exact same street name."

"This was my neighborhood. But it wasn't any regular neighborhood." Darrison was quiet for a minute before he opened his mouth to speak with sorrow. "This was my childhood."

Adrian scoffed.

"It's really not. I have to live here knowing that someone is probably waiting for me back in that neighborhood. But I can't bring myself to go back there if that person resents me for moving," Darrison said, tears welling up in his eyes. "I have the same dream when I fall asleep every night. That I'm back in my old neighborhood, preparing to move away. My best friend, looking at me with hatred and disbelief because I was leaving him."

"That's odd, I also lived on that street." Adrian looked up at Darrison. "Is that really you? Darrison Hougins?"

"Yeah, did I know you back then?" Darrison asked.

"Of course, how could you forget me? We were best friends."

"That was you?" Darrison said. "Who are you living with now?"

"After you moved away, my mother died. Then, my father abused me. I was forced to come live here with my aunt and uncle." Darrison wiped his tears and patted Adrian's back, "I'm not mad at you. Don't worry about it. I just can't believe we're together again after so long."

After they finished their project, Darrison returned home. The next day, Darrison was once late again for his English class. He sprinted down the hall and turned the corridor. Then he slowly opened the door to his class.

"Come in, Darrison. Just sit down," Mrs. Cherry said.

He walked over to Adrian and sat down in the empty seat.

"Please turn in your collaborative writing," Mrs. Cherry said. Students shuffled through the piles of papers and bags. Adrian and Darrison were proud of theirs and turned it in.

Darrison looked over at Adrian, "Hey, you want to join me at lunch?"

"Wouldn't I be bothering you?" Adrian said. "After all I did shove you at school last week. I'm basically the bully that everyone hates."

"Well," Darrison said, "that can change."

Adrian smiled for what seemed like the first time in a long time.

The boys walked down the hallway toward the cafeteria together.

# BELOVED LOST

## By Christine Ha

I closed my empty eyes.
In front of me stood a single figure.
She caressed my face with her cold hands,
her rouge lips smiled back at me.
I walked alongside her,
toward the benevolent sunset,
But despite the merciful scene,
silence resonated.

I opened my empty eyes.
In front of me, the broad line of the horizon.
Upset waves echoed below,
despite the cold stone beneath my feet,
I stood alone.
Silent tears fell,
Trickling down a young woman's
slate grave.

# THAT ONE BEAT

## By Cheyenne Danielle Hunt

Beating at the pulse
Symbolizing life
Sweet simplicity
That One Beat

It starts with a heart
Or two
That One Beat cements in your veins
Symbolizing Life

Exposure perceives
That smile of an angel
That One Beat is a haven of her insecurities
With the misery of her past is now buried
Symbolizing Strength

Like That One Beat of a song
Emotions are tied to it
The influence of emotions
The coinciding voice of a methodical beat
That One Beat of her song
Is his heart
That One Beat. . .
Is her music
That One Beat. . .
Is indispensable to her soul

# THE SUN

## By Tuyet Duong

At the start of the day,
I'd wake up and say,
It'll be better this way.

The sun will continue to rise,
Each day comes a new surprise
Reminding all to stay wise.

Let the sun shine bright,
Making every moment right,
As everyone holds you tight.

Let the sun come out from the clouds,
Allow it to make you feel proud
Of every word you shout aloud.

Remember to stand tall.
Don't let anyone break your wall.
Even if you feel you've lost it all.

There's always sun after the rain.
Let it wash away all of the pain
And give you more to gain.

As the sun begins to set,
Remember to never forget
Everything you have as of yet.

# THE CRYSTAL CHASE

## By Jenny Nguyen

"YOU'LL NEVER GET ME to tell you where the jewels are," the thief mocked from behind a fruit stand.

"You pretentious fool," Paris glared at him with murderous eyes. "If you don't tell me where they are, I'll kill you."

The man threw back his head and laughed. "Threatening me won't work...but a small price of 10,000 gold can."

"Curse you!" Paris slammed the rack with his fist in frustration, causing apples and pears to tumble onto the grassy road from the fruit stand. "I bought those jewels fairly with my hard-earned money. How dare you rob them from me."

"I find; I keep," the thief said in an indifferent tone and propped up his bare feet, covered in tattoos and adorned with a ankle bracelet, atop the table. "Now move aside. I have customers to deal with. Unless you'd like to bargain for your precious treasure?"

Paris narrowed his eyes at the thief. "Is this even your stand? I thought I saw someone else at this table. You probably stole the poor owner's money too."

Before the thief could open his mouth, a woman's cry cut through the crowd.

Paris spun around to find a plump, red-faced woman dressed in an apron pointing at the thief. Two city guards stood on either side of her.

"That's the man who put a sleeping potion in my drink before stealing my stand," she yelled.

"Get him." The guards charged towards the man.

"Time for me to leave." The thief threw off his stolen apron and pulled a brown shawl over himself. "Nice stealing from you, adieu!" He threw a small object at the ground which burst into light blue smoke that filled the stand. It smelled of cotton candy and burnt ash.

Paris coughed and waved the smoke away. Down the road, people shrieked as the thief pushed passed them and knocked down crates of produce to block his trail. Paris clenched his fists before leaping into the crowd. The man jumped over broken boxes of cabbages and slipped past people like a fish. Paris narrowed his eyes at the bobbing brown shawl in front of him, trying to keep from losing his target in the crowd.

The thief looked over his shoulder and grinned. "You're going to have to do better than that to catch me," he called out.

Paris furrowed his brows and increased his speed. The thief ran up a makeshift stairway of haystacks and leapt onto the back of a moving horse cart filled with flour bags.

Paris followed close behind but was almost too late--he landed with a pained groan at the back of the cart with only his upper body strength to keep himself from falling. He wrapped his arms over the furthest wall at the back of the cart as it rode through the town.

"You cannot seem to get enough of me, can you?" The thief rose to his feet and dusted off white flour from his clothes. His chest heaved from the chase, and sweat painted his dark brow. He approached Paris and lifted a foot to kick him off. Paris clenched his teeth and growled. When the thief's foot came down, Paris's hand shot out to wrap around his leg. He lost grip from the side of the cart, and the two came tumbling down off the cart in a swarm of dust and flour.

Paris landed on his back with a grunt before rolling upright to find the thief scrambling to his feet and holding his side with a pained expression. He launched himself at the thief with his fists raised. The man stumbled backwards and pulled something shiny out of his robe. People nearby screamed and ran away. Paris stopped in his tracks and eyed him cautiously.

"You are annoying, you know that?" the man said in a scornful tone as he pointed the dagger at Paris. When he spat at the ground, his saliva was tinged with blood.

In the distance, the sound of the guards clambering down the road caught their attention. The thief cursed and grabbed a random girl from the fleeing crowd. She screamed as he put the dagger to her neck.

"Unhand her," Paris demanded.

"I'm not going to hurt her as long as you let me go," he said. Paris narrowed his eyes. Despite the calm in the thief's voice, sweat beaded his forehead and his hand trembled as he held the weapon. Paris took a step forward.

A flash of frustration crossed the thief's face. "Do you think I'm lying? I'll kill her if you get too close. Stay back!" When he pressed the knife harder to the girl's throat, she fainted.

"See here, the guards will be here any minute," Paris said. "If you tell me where the jewels are and give back the money you stole, I'll let you escape. Deal?" He held out his hand.

The yells of the guards were getting louder and louder. Their heavy boots pounded against the dirt road like falling rocks. The thief glared at the man with distrustful eyes, but he knew he didn't have much of a choice. He needed to get out alive.

He cursed and shoved the unconscious girl forward. Paris lunged forward and caught her in his arms. Gold coins scattered all over the floor as the thief emptied his pockets.

"Meet me at the water canals at nightfall. Alone," he said.

"How do I know you'll be there?"

The thief grinned. A golden tooth shined in his smile. "You have my word. If that even means anything to you coming from a beggar. But you saved my life." He backed up into the shadows of the street and pulled his shawl over his head. "I may be a thief, but I keep my promises. Farewell." The man ran off into a narrow alleyway and disappeared into the anonymity of the crowds.

Paris watched the thief escape as the city guards caught up.

"Where did that thief go?" They panted. "Did he return everything he stole?"

"Almost everything." He carefully carried the girl over to one of the guards. The possibilities and uncertainties of the night filled his mind. Who was this man? Would he stick to his word? Paris made his way home, his mind heavy with anticipation.

The nightfall was warm and quiet. Water trickled along their course towards the farmlands beyond the city walls, and the dark sky was full of stars. Paris waited by the canal with his gloved hands resting on the handle of his sword at his side. His light metal armor gleamed in the moonlight and the occasional breeze rustled through his brown hair. He was beginning to regret letting the thief go until the sound of footsteps caught his attention.

"I didn't know you were a knight," the familiar voice said.

Paris turned to find the thief with his hands in his pockets and a cheeky grin spread across his face. He gestured to the sword at Paris's side. "Did you really have to bring that?"

"Better to be safe than to be sorry," Paris said. "The jewels?"

"Ah, yes." The man reached inside his robes, still grinning. Paris lifted a brow. This man was always grinning as if he was in on some secret joke. He probably didn't even bring the jewels. He might even be reaching for a weapon now. How could Paris be so foolish as to--"Here it is."

Paris's eyes widened as the man pulled out a dazzling necklace full of crystals out of his robe. It gleamed under the moonlight like hand-held stars, a true beauty to behold.

"Why do you look so surprised? I told you I keep my promises," the thief said and held the precious necklace out towards Paris. Paris reached out in disbelief.

He expected the thief to attack him, but nothing happened as he took the necklace and put it back into the safety of his satchel.

"Thank you," Paris said. "To be honest, I didn't expect you to come."

"And I didn't expect you to spare me earlier. But here we are." The man laughed and spun around with a flourish of his ragged robes. Paris found himself smiling as well.

"Well, today was fun. Now I must go and steal--I mean *borrow* some other things from other people," he said.

"Is that something you should be telling a knight of the Royal Guard?" Paris asked.

"Not to worry. I have reformed my ways," the man declared. He then bowed deeply before Paris. "I must bid you goodbye. Thank you for your kindness. Farewell, strange knight!" He then spun on his heel and retreated into the darkness of the night.

Before he was gone, Paris called after him. "The name's Paris. Who are you?"

The thief stopped in his tracks and was silent for a moment. His dark silhouette shifted as his head turned over his shoulder, but Paris could only see shadows.

"Me? What's in a name but a poor expectation for whom the bearer must live up to? Call me what you like, but we shall meet again soon. Goodbye, Paris." And with that, the thief disappeared into the shadows.

Paris stood alone at the water's edge and clutched his satchel. What a strange man. What made him think they'd meet again? Paris hoped their next encounter would be far better than their first.

He retraced his way home and tapped his finger against the hilt of his sword to the beat of an old song he was humming, feeling glad and relieved he had no use for it that night.

\* \* \*

"Honey, I'm home," Paris called as he entered a small cottage.

"Daddy!" A little girl with brown hair and emerald eyes jumped up to greet him. He laughed and pulled her up into his arms.

"So you finally decided to return home." A young woman with raven hair appeared through a kitchen doorway with a hand on her hip. Her green eyes gleamed like a cat's and her lips tilted up in a calm smile.

Paris smiled and kissed her on the cheek. "You look beautiful as ever, Cynthia. And I was out catching the thief I told you about earlier. Do you remember?"

"Did you get him?" She asked. Paris averted his eyes.

"No...not really. I let him go," he said.

Cynthia rose a brow. "You're too soft, Paris. People don't change unless you hold a whip behind them. That whip is the law, and you're the one who's supposed to be holding it." She scolded.

"People can change if you show compassion and love for them once in a while." Paris replied and kissed his daughter's cheek. "Most people don't want to do wrong. They just need someone to believe in their ability to do right."

His wife gave him a rueful smile. "You give people too much credit."

Paris winked at her. "And you give people too little." He then set his daughter on the ground. "Alright Anna, off to bed you go. No whining."

"Come along, sweetie." Cynthia took her daughter's hand and led her through a dim hallway. When his wife and daughter disappeared into the bedrooms, Paris eased down into a chair and began taking off his armor. The satchel carrying the necklace hung at his side and he smiled as he imagined his wife's joyful face when he presented it to her.

"Hey, Cynthia, can you come here for a bit?" He said when she returned. Her eyebrows knit together in concern.

"What is it? Are you hurt?" she asked and came to his side.

His gloved hands shook with excitement as he pulled the gleaming necklace from the cloth bag. Cynthia's face lit up with surprise as her eyes fell upon the jeweled beauty. Even in the dim light, the crystals sparkled like stars.

"Is this for me?" Cynthia asked with awe-stricken eyes. "How did you get this?"

Paris smiled from ear to ear. "Pure crystals from the islands of Fantasia, got it from a foreign merchant during Market Day. Saved up all my gold for months to buy you this." He turned her around and began to fasten it around her neck. "Do you like it?"

"I love it," she breathed. "It's so beautiful." When she turned back around, tears glimmered in her eyes.

"It looks gorgeous on you." Paris said, his eyes full of love.

Cynthia smiled and wrapped her arms around him. "I love you so much, Paris."

He pulled her closer to him and kissed her head. "I love you too, Cynthia. You are the world to me." For a moment, they just stood there, basking in each other's love and warmth in comfortable silence. Until Cynthia began to squirm in his arms.

Paris let her go and looked at her in confusion. "Is something wrong?"

"No, it's just that…" She made a face and began to scratch her neck. "I suddenly feel very itchy right now." Her scratching began to increase in intensity as the seconds went by. "Oh my God, Paris, what's on this necklace?" She cried.

"What, there's nothing wrong with it." Paris said and fumbled to unlatch it from her neck. He then pulled off one glove and touched the jewels with his bare fingers. At first, he felt nothing. A couple seconds later, a warm sensation filled his entire hand and an incredible itchiness overtook him.

"What in the world?" He cried as he began to scratch himself with the other hand. Paris bent down to examine the necklace, and found that it was lathered in some strange, clear sap that he had mistaken earlier for gloss. The truth dawned upon him like a slap in the face.

"That damn weasel!"

"What are you talking about?" Cynthia said as she continued to scratch her neck.

"I was chasing the thief today because he stole the necklace. He promised to give it back to me but he must have rubbed poison ivy sap all over it as a joke." Paris grabbed the necklace with his gloved hand and put it back into its satchel. He cursed himself for not inspecting the jewels earlier before giving it to Cynthia.

"Poison ivy? You've got to be kidding me," Cynthia said and rushed to the kitchen. "Hurry, we need to wash ourselves off."

Paris groaned as he got to his feet and followed her. He could almost hear the thief laughing at him from miles away.

# SHE

## By Vylan Tran

SHE WANTS TO BE LOVED,
Love is important to her.
SHE DOESN'T KNOW HOW
Yet she feels useless.
SHE LUSTS FOR THINGS,
Wonders if she's good enough
SHE WILL FIGHT FOR YOU,
But she's too weak
SHE WANTS TO FEEL SPECIAL,
Only you can make her feel that way.
SHE IS WILLING TO GIVE UP EVERYTHING,
Just to be happy with you.
SHE CRIES,
Hoping you will comfort her.
SHE WILL PLACE HER TRUST IN YOU, LOVE YOU,
Just don't betray her.
SHE WANTS YOU IN HER LIFE.
And only you.
I AM SHE.

# A PERFECT MORNING

## By Chloe Shane Sanchez

The night is dark,
Tinted with an onyx shade.
Trees glisten as the rain patters down on them.
With clouds painted a crimson color,
The bedroom glooming with magenta night light,
The people comfort themselves in the darkness.

Then an arctic lightning strikes that brightens the road--
The rain stops.
The clouds fade into their normal slate color,
The moon shines down on pine-colored leaves,
covered with rain drops.

Though, people ignore it
as they continue to sleep
before tangerine-colored sun rays that shine down,
signaling a perfect morning.

# COLD

## By Helen Nguyen

She used to tell me how my hands were cold,
How she loved to give me warmth with her hold,
The way her body enveloped my own,
As I slept unaware of the unknown.
My lips pressed against her pulse,
I could not feel her heartbeat,
I should have taken it as a sign.
I saw galaxies upon her skin,
My fingers tracing freckled stars on her chin,
Yet she saw that our stars weren't aligned,
What we had met a flat line.
After she left the next morning,
I found myself mourning.
Her love became a ghost,
And she took my mind as a host,
Haunting my thoughts,
Leaving me yearning for feeling
that can no longer be sought.

# SEASONAL CHANGE

### By Joseph Ho

The daffodil sun
nowhere to be seen
Under the gray gloomy mist.

Lilac flowers glow on green grass
Clouds transform the bright sky
into shade with a cold breeze.

Hickory trees stand in the dark
The forest is quiet
as the cold winds blows by.

Animals unseen with winter approaching.
Soon the silent and windy forest
will be covered in porcelain snow.

# ALL IN A DAY'S WORK

## By Derek Nguyen

"WHATEVER PLAN YOU HAVE in mind, make it quick." The man looked in the truck's rearview mirror and spotted hooded men pushing through the crowd. "Uh, we have a problem Macie."

The woman looked over her shoulder and cursed. "I thought we lost--oh never mind. Jeremiah, there should be a weapons crate in the back. I need you to hold them off while I get this damned thing to start." She turned the keys, and the engine made a hollow rattle before sputtering out.

"You sure did come prepared," Jeremiah said as he clambered onto the truck's back. He flipped open the lid, peered inside, and smiled. He pulled out a Thompson and slapped a magazine into the receiver. "Where did you find all this?"

"Now is not the time." The engine made a hacking cough and died again. "They're getting closer."

Jeremiah turned to see the hooded men step into the market square, their eyes scanning the bustling scene. "It's all right, they don't see us." There was a metallic glint in the corner of his eye, and he turned to the left to see a knife hurtling towards him. He ducked, and it ripped through the tarp where his head had been moments before. The assailant stepped out of the alleyway, a revolver in his hand. Jeremiah pulled the trigger, and the man crumpled, his brown shirt blooming with crimson.

The others turned at the sound of the gunshot and yelled obscenities as they charged the truck. Jeremiah sighed and lifted up the Thompson. "Guess they know now."

Dirt kicked up as bullets tore through the ground and the men dove aside to avoid the hailstorm of bullets. Wood splintered and fruits exploded into orange, yellow, and red mist as Jeremiah tore the marketplace apart. "Anytime now, I've got to reload soon."

"Almost there," Macie said. "I just need to adjust…"

A shadow flickered across the skylight above, and a man landed on the truck's hood and aimed his pistol at Macie. Glass shattered into powder as she ducked to avoid the shots. Jeremiah turned and sprayed a burst with the Thompson, knocking the man off the hood. Macie nodded in thanks before turning the keys again. The truck roared as the engine came to life. "Hold on, I'm cutting it close."

Jeremiah frowned at her. "Wait you can't be—" The truck lurched backward and spun in a donut, smashing into market stands and kicking up clouds of red dust. Jeremiah flew face-first onto the opposite side. Regaining his balance, he groaned. "Of course you were serious."

"I said, hold on." Macie stamped on the accelerator, launching the truck into the wall of gunmen. Bullets whizzed and metal shrieked as the truck became riddled with holes. It roared out of the marketplace with Jeremiah firing from the back as they sped off.

As the desert town shrank to a white speck, he turned to smile at Macie. "All things considered, that didn't go half bad." He leaned back and rubbed his face. "We almost died, I've got a purple welt on my forehead, and the truck wants to give out at any moment. But the important thing is that we've got the idol. All in a day's work."

Macie looked at the golden idol in the passenger seat. "Why would they go through all this trouble to keep this away from us? The museum deserves to have a few relics of history."

Jeremiah shrugged and pulled out a canteen. "Oh, I don't know," he said between gulps. "Maybe it has something to do with it being a piece of an unknown civilization? Must fetch a hefty price in the black market."

"For an artifact we've just found, you sure do know a lot about it."

"What can I say?" He closed his canteen and wiped off the droplets of water on his chin. "Working as an archaeological mercenary for ten years does have its perks." Jeremiah stared out into the yellow dunes, squinting his eyes at the horizon. "When did we get a tail?"

Macie flashed a glance at the rear view mirror and her eyes widened. A trail of grey and tan dots passed over a dune, kicking up sand as they tore through the landscape. "Who are they?"

Jeremiah peered at the specks and shook his head. He pulled out a sniper rifle from the weapons crate and flashed a look at Macie before aiming it. "Want the good news or bad news?"

"Always bad news first."

"Bad news is that our tail is made of military jeeps and motorcycles. It looks like Adrian Falcone is at the head. As for the good news, well there's none."

Macie cursed and looked at Jeremiah. "Who is this Adrian? Some kind of tomb raider?" He turned and made a grim smile.

"He runs an entire tomb raiding business down here. He's the one that's been giving museum expeditions so much trouble." Jeremiah frowned. "He doesn't take too kindly to those who take his loot. Even if it was yours to begin with."

She reached under her seat and pulled out a sawed-off shotgun before setting it beside her. "Get ready for a fight. Can you pick off anyone from this distance?"

"I sure can. But first you have to come to a stop, it's hard to shoot accurately in this truck." Seeing her frown, he rolled his eyes. "That means no, if you were wondering."

She eyed the rear view mirror, watching the specks grow into the outlines of vehicles. They leaped over the dunes and onto the road behind the truck. "When can I ever get a clean break?"

"By keeping me alive."

"Thanks for reminding me." A crack rang across the sky, and the rear view mirror shattered. She turned to look at the jeeps bearing down on their truck. "They almost killed me from a bouncing jeep going at fifty, and you can't even land a shot close to them from a truck moving at thirty-five?"

Jeremiah glared at her. "Not all mercenaries are gifted in the art of sniping. I'll see what I can do." He peered into the scope and straightened up. Taking deep breaths, he ignored the shots flying through the air and closed one eye. The rifle kicked back into his shoulder, and Macie could see a dust cloud rise up from among the pack of jeeps.

Jeremiah whistled. "Well what do you know. I nailed the driver right in the chest, sent everyone onboard to their maker." The rifle cracked once more, and he chuckled. "Hit nothing but blue sky that time." He swapped the sniper rifle for the Thompson. "I'm more of an up-close-and-personal kind of guy if you haven't figured it out yet."

"Your snarky jokes can wait. Adrian's pack of wolves are here." Macie stomped on the gas pedal and eyed the steam rising out of the engine bay. "I can't put too much stress on this truck or it'll blow the engine. It's back to guard duty, Jeremiah."

"When isn't it?"

"What did I just say about the snark?" A thunderclap split the air and sparks bounced off of the truck's side. "Damn, where did that come from?" Peering over the window, she saw a motorcycle jump over a dune and land on the road. Its driver aimed a lever action shotgun at the cargo bay and fired, tearing a hole in the gray tarp.

The Thompson roared, kicking up sand and striking the motorcycle's front wheel. Its driver tumbled over with a drawn out scream as he was crushed by the weight of the falling bike. Jeremiah rose up from where he had been crouching. "You're welcome."

"Save that for later, here comes the rest of the gang."

Behind them, the first tan jeep roared into view, its machine gun roaring to life. Jeremiah retaliated with short bursts, striking sparks on its hood. "Keep swerving, Macie. If a bullet punctures a tire we're cooked." The jeep surged forward under fire again. Jeremiah hugged the floor, bullets parting the air above him. He squeezed off another burst, and the jeep's gunner fell with a short grunt before rolling on the dusty road.

Its driver scowled and swerved aside before pulling up to the truck's cab. The man next to him stood up to jump, then jerked backward as he met a cluster of shotgun pellets. Macie racked the pump and pulled off another blast, disintegrating the driver's horrified face. His body slumped to the left, pulling the jeep sideways to block the road. A biker that was dueling with Jeremiah swerved too late and was launched skyward in a rain of sparks and bike parts.

Another jeep leaped across the dunes and onto the road, its occupants crouching to avoid the Thompson's bullets. Jeremiah growled and pulled the trigger again, his heart dropping when the gun refused to fire. "A jam? Out of all the damned times…"

A bullet ripped through the tarp beside him as a raider dove onto the truck. Jeremiah fired his sidearm at the same time as his opponent and both men's guns flew out of their hands in a cascade of sparks. They drew knives and charged, slashing and hacking at each other. Jeremiah stumbled over his pistol, and the raider dived forward. Jeremiah blocked the blade with his own, struggling to keep the silver point from piercing his eye. Out of the corner of his vision he saw the jeep's gunner aim at his head. "Macie!"

The truck stopped, and the jeep rammed into the rear. Macie cursed and stepped on the gas, causing the men in the back of the truck to fly into the jeep. Glass shattered as they were launched through its windshield and onto the back. The gunner sidestepped to avoid the flailing men and lost his balance on a crate of ammunition before falling with a rain of brass onto the cracked asphalt. Blood arced across the air as the driver took shots at Jeremiah, grazing his shoulder and cheek.

Jeremiah dove into the passenger seat to avoid the bullets and kicked the driver. Hardened leather met skin, and the man tumbled on the ground. The other raider dove at him, a gleaming hunting knife in hand. Punching skywards, Jeremiah carried the man over his head and onto the hood. Scrabbling for a handhold, the raider was pulled under with a yelp, and the jeep bounced up with a nauseating crunch.

Climbing into the driver's seat, Jeremiah looked over his shoulder. Two bikes flashed past him, not bothering to open fire. "Am I not dangerous enough for you?" Bullets ricocheted off the armored panels, and a low wheezing started as a rear wheel ruptured. He smiled, pulling out a kukri from the inside of his shirt. "There you are, Adrian."

Jeremiah slammed on the brakes and leaped sideways. The last jeep roared by, firing its machine gun. He landed with a grunt on the back, reaching for something to pull himself up with. Stars appeared in his eyes as the gunner kicked Jeremiah in the head. His arm flashed out, pulling the gunner off his feet. Vaulting himself up, Jeremiah kicked the gunner off in return, forcing the raider to grab onto the jeep's bumper to stay on.

A gunshot pierced the chaos, and Jeremiah's left arm burned as a bullet ripped through his bicep. He stumbled towards the passenger to dodge the gunshots and knocked the rifle out of the man's hand with a slash of his kukri. A thrust sent the curved blade hurtling towards the man's chest. Metal clanged as Jeremiah's blade was stopped short by another kukri. "You have good taste in weapons, Adrian. Now if only you had good manners."

The man scowled. "Jokes won't save you." A jab followed by an uppercut launched Jeremiah backwards. Spikes shot up through his left arm as the full weight of his body fell on it. Gasping, he rolled over in time to dodge Adrian's diving stab. The blade left a long cut along Jeremiah's right cheek as it smashed into the metal floor.

Sweeping his leg out, he knocked Adrian over. He jabbed downwards with his kukri, but Adrian caught his hand, twisting the blade back towards Jeremiah. Pushing himself upwards, Adrian loomed over him, the silver blade inching towards his neck. "That was good. But not good enough."

Jeremiah chuckled. "How about this?" He let go of the knife and twisted sideways, feeling the hilt slam into the floor where his neck was a second ago. As Adrian struggled to pull it out, Jeremiah kneed him in the groin. The raider howled and stumbled backwards, gasping for breath. "Was that better?"

Adrian roared and drew out his pistol. His hand jerked upwards as Jeremiah dove forwards, pushing the gun away. "Just give up. There's no use fighting me."

"Are you sure, Adrian? It seems that you're out of luck." Seeing his eyes flick downwards Jeremiah turned to see the gunner clamber back on, a pistol aimed at his back.

Adrian sneered, spitting in his face. "Oh how the tables have tur-"

Jeremiah dashed forward, and a moment later Adrian was tumbling against another body. Tasting sand in his mouth, he rose as the jeep sped off. He aimed his pistol at Jeremiah's shrinking figure, but then holstered it. "Fool won't know what hit him."

Jeremiah saluted Adrian and then wrenched his kukri out of the floor. "Don't you even dare-" He turned around to see an empty jeep. Hearing heavy thumping, he saw the driver rolling alongside the road. "Huh, I'd never thought he would chicken out of a fight."

Stamping on the accelerator Jeremiah raced towards the truck. Gunshots peppered the silence, but he couldn't tell if it was from Macie or the bikers. As he neared the battle, one of them glanced sideways and dropped back. "You want to tango, buddy?" He revved up the engine. "Well, you've got a partner."

Pellets split the air as the biker opened fire, veering sideways to avoid the charging jeep. Jeremiah cursed as they struck the engine, causing light gray smoke to rise out from the grill. Looking over his shoulder he saw the raider flip the shotgun to reload. Slamming on the brakes, he felt the pellets fly overhead and shatter the windshield into a cascade of glass. The biker zoomed by, turning around to repeat the cycle.

"Persistent little bugger aren't you?" He rifled through the glove compartment on the passenger side. "Well now," Jeremiah said as he pulled out a lever action shotgun, "things just got more interesting." The bike's whine grew louder, and the front of the jeep sparked as the biker took another potshot at him. Jeremiah growled and returned fire, striking the ground right behind the raider. "Damn it, hold still and make my job easier."

The biker circled back, exchanging fire with him again. Acrid black smoke began to billow out of the front now, making Jeremiah's eyes water. Flipping the shotgun to reload it, he eyed the gray speck that grew larger as the bike charged him again. Settling the gun on the windshield frame, he leaned down, using the smoke as cover.

The biker growled and aimed at the driver's seat. He pulled the trigger, and the wave of pellets parted the air, revealing empty air. As he passed by the jeep, he saw Jeremiah hugging the dashboard, a shotgun aimed right at him.

Jeremiah fired, and the pellets struck the man square in the chest. The limp body slumped down, then rolled off as the bike fell over. Jeremiah stopped the jeep and staggered over to the bike. "I need a vacation," he muttered as he righted it. "These wounds aren't going away anytime soon."

The truck was out of sight now, but the trail of empty shotgun shells, spots of blood, and smoking wreckage of a motorbike were easy enough to follow. Passing by the totaled bike, Jeremiah noticed that the man pinned underneath it was still alive. Slowing to a stop, he limped over to him.

Jeremiah peered down at the raider. "Rough day, isn't it?" His eyes fluttered open, and he groaned.

The man wheezed. "I don't recognize…is that you Adrian?" Jeremiah kneeled down, noting the pool of dark red seeping out from his gut.

"What are--" He hesitated. His nose crinkled from the foul fumes that rose from the leaking gasoline. "Yes, it's me Adrian."

The man spat in Jeremiah's face and shook his head in a delirious daze. "Curse you. You told us that they were just museum workers. You didn't mention that one of them was…" He doubled up and coughed out blood. Wheezing, the man went limp. "Our own…."

"What the…" Jeremiah stood up scratching his head. "Our own? What in the world is he talking about?" Hearing a rattling engine he turned around to see a battered truck moving towards him.

"Wow, you survived." Macie hopped out of the truck, holstering her shotgun. "For a moment I thought you were one of the raiders." She eyed the distant smoking wreckage. "You did all that?"

"I guess…" Jeremiah looked down at the dead raider. "This man…he said something that didn't make sense." He eyed Macie, glancing at the shotgun in her holster.

Her eyes narrowed. "What did he say?"

Jeremiah lowered his hand towards his own shotgun. "He said one of us--"

They both drew their weapons, aiming at each other's heads. Other than the light rustle of the desert breeze, there was no sound. Jeremiah snorted, rolling his eyes in disbelief.

"Out of all the…you're with the raiders?"

Macie narrowed her eyes. "Correction, I was with the raiders." She smiled, nodding at the dead biker. "I canceled my contract early, decided that the idol could be my last earning. Adrian didn't like that idea."

"So you were never an archaeologist, the more you know…" Jeremiah sighed. "Do we really have to do this? I mean we're both mercenaries, can't we be sensible people and split the money?" He assumed a nonchalant stance, eying Macie's shotgun. "We don't need things to get--"

Thunder echoed across the dunes, rumbling through the ground. A few pellets grazed Macie's shoulder, causing her to jerk sideways. She cursed and looked back to where Jeremiah lay crumpled in a pool of blood. Macie knelt over him, sneering at his glazed eyes. "Sorry, but I had to end my contract with you too." He shifted his head to look at her, his unfocused eyes becoming clear again.

"Same to you." His arm flashed upwards, stabbing the kukri into Macie's abdomen. She gasped, her shaking hands grabbing the blade in an attempt to pull it out. Jeremiah stood up, using his weight to push it in further. Once it was hilt-deep in her gut, he shoved her onto the ground.

Pointing at his bleeding arm Jeremiah said, "I've been shot here twice today. I don't know how you missed, better luck next time. If you believe in reincarnation that is." He tore off the sleeves from his shirt and began wrapping them around the wounds. Looking at her, he knelt down and pulled the kukri out before wiping it on his shirt. "You forced my hand. I'm sorry it came to this." He looked up at the cloudless azure sky. "You could've started fresh. Such a waste."

Macie shifted her head to face him, shuddering from the effort. "I should've known this would be the death of me..." Her body convulsed, and a gurgling sound rose from her throat. Jeremiah waited for the breathing to stop, then closed her eyes.

"See you on the other side." He slumped his shoulders and sighed. "Maybe I should begin applying for solo contracts, these co-op ones never work out well." He got into the truck, leaning into the driver's seat to catch his ragged breaths. Looking over at the passenger seat, he grabbed the golden idol.

"Are you happy now?" He frowned at the large smile etched on its face. "Everything's gone to shambles, and I'm here talking to a figurine." Feeling its huge ruby eyes bore into his skull, he shuddered and tossed it back onto the seat. "I used to think cursed treasure was baloney. Not anymore." He looked away from the idol. "You inflict greed on everything you lay eyes on. I should throw you in the sand, but greed will lead me back to you anyways." Shaking his head, he turned on the engine. "I'm becoming cynical already. Perfect."

A glint bounced off the side mirror, blinding him for a moment. "What the?" He turned around and saw a jeep kicking up dust in the distance. Cursing, he began reloading the shotgun. "Already cursed by the damn idol. Can't get a clean break at all. But then again, I never did believe in clean breaks. All in a day's work I guess." Leaning down, he listened to the rumbling. It ground to a halt, and he could hear heavy footsteps. Taking a deep breath, he listened as the sound of boots on gravel grew louder. They neared the truck, then stopped by Macie's corpse.

Jeremiah rose over the door, aiming at the darkened figure. Thunderclaps echoed across the dunes, fading into silence once again. The truck's door opened, and he stepped out, waving the shotgun in an arc. He saw Adrian's body on the road and walked over to it.

"Was it worth the trouble? You've got nothing to show for it." The raider's glazed blue eyes stared back at him. Jeremiah snapped his fingers and went back to the truck.

"Here you go." He returned with the golden idol and set it beside Adrian's body. "Consider that as compensation for your troubles." Jeremiah aimed the shotgun at the idol and pulled the trigger. It shattered into chunks of gold and jewel dust, leaving one ruby intact.

He picked it up and pocketed it. "Good day to you Adrian." Jeremiah tipped an imaginary hat and walked back to the truck. "All in a day's work."

# BALLER

## By Colleen Nguyen

Sweat drips down your face as everything begins to slow.
There are people in front of you, sluggish, their arms above their heads.
Your breathing quickens,
Your heart pounds against your chest,
A reassuring heaviness on your hand comes and goes.
As the ball hits the ground,
A satisfying thud bounces off, rhythmic and quick.
You take a deep breath,
Your view becomes crisp and clear,
The noises around you stop. Silence.
With steady hands you hold the ball,
Then you throw.

You watch, eyes wide
The ball makes its way through the air,
Against the backboard,
Into the hoop with a swish,
And then everything comes rushing back.

# OBSESSION

## By Huan Dao

Her soft lips take your breath away,
Is this a nightmare that will never end?
Or a dream that you never want to end?
She holds you tight,
She will never let you go.
Is this the true love that
They've always been talking about?
You feel that she is the one,
The one that you would watch the sunset fall with,
Share your deepest secrets with,
Without them judging you in the slightest,
To wake up seeing her beside you.
Is that too much to ask?
When she comes up to you
The dream shatters
She only wants one thing
Separation.

You fall on your knees,
From all the pain in the world
Her?
Why?
The person you love so much
"What have I done" you cry.
The pictures on the wall,
You hold back your tears,
This will be okay.
Sure it will be
Flowers will bloom
Pain will heal
You tell yourself this every night
Especially tonight.

The stench of gasoline overpowers
The strong smell of her perfume
That she left in this room
The lighter on the nightstand
It has always been there
Flickering, flickering
The fire shines through the dark room
The gasoline and matches
They're soul mates
Just like you and her
It takes over the night
And the room
The black smoke engulfs the room.

She is tied up.
Screaming for help
You stand here
Wondering where she was when you needed her the most
You wish you could help her
But how
Pain will heal though, right?
You hope so,
At least you hope so.
When her burnt, lifeless body
No longer responds
She will eventually say "I love you" again, right?
In hell
Where she belongs

# DON'T FORGET CHARLIE

## By Peter Vu

When I first met you,
I knew you were the one.
The way you made me laugh every day,
The way you made me smile every day,
I just knew you were the perfect friend.
You were there for me when I was at my lowest,
You were the reason why I was at my highest.
I couldn't get enough of your love and friendship.
We would always go to each other's houses late at night
And early in the morning just to pass the time.
When we were unable to see each other,
We called.
You were more than just a friend,
You were my Brother.
Some days we'd ignore each other because we didn't think the same.
But after a while, you were sent away.
At that moment I knew,
I didn't have anyone to make me smile anymore,
I didn't have anyone to make me laugh anymore,
I didn't have anyone to receive love and friendship from anymore,
I didn't have anyone's house to go to anymore,
I didn't have anyone to call anymore,
I didn't have anyone at all anymore.
I understand that everything falls apart,
but I wish it didn't for you.
I understand that people come and go,
But I wish it didn't for you.
No matter what happens,
You will always be my Brother.

# WHY CAN'T I?

## By Vylan Tran

She stands in the doorway,
Hair drenched in water.
Her eyes tear up,
Rain pours harder,
She takes off her shoes and coat,
Closing the door, slowly.

She places her forehead on the door,
Wondering what she did wrong,
Wondering why?
Why can't she do anything right?

Slowly bending her knees,
Hitting on the ground,
She hugs her legs and cries.
Lights flicker,
Her chin rests against her arms,
She looks at the wooden floor,
Asking,
"Why can't I?"

# INFATUATION
## By Angelina Ngo

I did something I never thought I would do,
I held you close.
In fear that I would lose you,
I held your hand.
As if you were leaving me once again,
I laid a kiss on your lips,
Afraid that it would be the something
I would truly miss.

Early in the morning
As I lie in bed
I begin wondering if you still need me.
If you miss me the way I miss you,
If you still care for me as much as I care for you,
If you want me in your life as much as I do you,
If you crave my presence as much I crave you.

Several hours have gone by
As I lie awake at night
Wondering if
You still love me.
Because I,
I still love you.

# A MINOR FALL

## By Tyler Ta

As feathers in the sky twirls,
The sun glistens on the world.
From the open seas
To the land covered in trees.

A city bustles with open ports,
As soldiers on ships shout with retorts.
A farmer plows his property,
And a shepherd leads his sheep ably.

Yes, all is fine and all is well,
As nothing can be anymore swell.
Even the fisherman is especially vigorous.
Oh? Isn't that young Icarus?

# SUSPECT

## By Leianna Giryan

THE SKY TURNED BLACK, and stars sparkled as the moon lit the path back to my house. My friends thought it would be funny to play hide-and-go-seek in the corn fields even after our parents warned us about the legend of the scarecrow. Typical of them.

"Who." Eyes flashed in the trees. I jumped. Startled and panting, I glanced around the crops, hoping to see the shadows of my friends.

"Thomas?" I trudged past the family scarecrow, my legs trembling with each step. I turned my head to the side to avoid the scarecrow's sewn, empty eyes. It was like the scarecrow was watching something--watching me.

"Boo."

I jumped back, tripping.

"Were you scared, Jen? The scarecrow's just a legend." Thomas and Lily snickered.

"You jerks." I scowled.

Thomas reached down for my hand and lifted me up. "Chill," he said as I punched his shoulder. "It was just a prank, bro."

"Seriously?" I said.

"Yeah."

"*Just* a prank?" I raised my voice with each word. "I could've died." I glared at my so-called friends.

"Well--"

"I could've hit my head on the ground. Maybe broken something. Did you think about that?" I took a deep breath and dusted myself off.

"Good thing there was a pile of hay where you fell," Lily said.

"What?"

"Are you blind? There's a pile of hay right under you."

"I fell on hard dirt though." I looked down at my feet. Hay covered the base of my shoes. "Why is this here?" A crow cawed above us, encircling our location as though waiting for carrion. My friends and I looked up at the crow's figure, our bodies tense.

Thomas frowned. "Are you okay? Maybe you really *did* hit your head."

124

The wind stopped blowing. A feeling of nausea grew as the crow closed in, and the pungent smell of carrion flooded the air. My stomach clenched as we locked arms and stepped away. Sweat dripped down our foreheads and our pupils dilated.

Lily scanned the area a few times until she noticed something different. She nudged to the open field. We stared forward. The scarecrow was gone. In its place, a pile of dry dirt remained, flies hovering above it. Her eyes flicked at the shadows, and her breathing grew faster. "That's just a legend. There has to be a logical explanation for this--"

"We are in a horror movie, guys," Thomas said, throwing both his hands into the air.

"Dude, shut up." Lilly stepped on his foot. "It'll hear you."

Thomas yelped. "Hey, they're new shoes. Lay off, Missy." He stuck out his tongue. "I love getting a good fright. Let's see if this legend is true." A sly smile crept across his face.

Lily and I exchanged glances.

"You're an idiot." I released his grasp on my arm. I walked the opposite way, waving a peace sign high in the air. "Have fun," I yelled back to the lovebirds.

Leaves crunched as footsteps followed me. "Jen. Don't leave me with him." Lily grabbed my hand and we walked away from him. She jabbed me in the arm as I puckered my lips and made kissing noises. "There's nothing between us."

Minutes passed, but we couldn't find our way back to the house.

"I think we're lost," I said.

Lily glanced at me with a reassuring smile. "You got this. I mean it's your farm."

"I could've sworn this was the route back." I looked around. From the row of corn to my left, something sparkled reflecting the moonlight I grabbed Lily's hand. It was the scarecrow. And it had a knife.

"It's real!" We ran. "Speed up!" I released Lily's hand and turned down the next row, sprinting to the left then zig-zagging through ten other rows until I reached one of the old oak trees. I slouched down against it, panting. "Okay, Lily." I glanced around. "Lily?"

"Jen!" Lily's scream resonated through the field. There was a long pause after.

Then a scream, closer to me than the first. Another scream from a few feet away in the darkness and the sound of flesh being penetrated repeatedly. I crawled through the next two rows, peering around the stalk of some corn. A pool of crimson red surrounded the shadow of another figure. Holding back my scream, I watched as the figure walked back down the row, away from me. I must find Thomas. When I no longer heard any more sounds of crunching steps along the

125

dried grass, I crept closed to the body. As I passed Lily's corpse, I caught a glimpse of her wounds. Her body was almost unrecognizable. There were gashes on her neck, back, and her face was covered with warm blood.

Tears slipped down my face, but I continued to run. My heart pounded. Groans echoed in the distance to my right. I weaved through the corn, scraping my skin along the drying leaving. I rushed to the source of the groans. My hand covered my mouth when I arrived. "Thomas…what happened?"

Hunched over, Thomas stumbled a few steps, coughed up blood and fell to the ground. "Man, I love frights." His wounds gushed blood. I dropped to the ground and cradled his head in my lap. Tears blurred my vision. "Where's Lily?" Thomas moved his head around.

"She's hiding," I lied. His breathing slowed. "You'll be okay…" He inhaled one last time. "Don't worry." His heart stopped, and he went limp in my arms.

My fingers curled into a fist, and my jaw clenched. Somebody or *something* had killed my friends. Why? I spotted our split rail fence. The "No Trespassing" sign mocked me in the darkness. I ripped it off the wooden post and twisted the board in half, stomping it with my boot into the hard-packed dirt. "I'll avenge you both. I won't rest until that is done."

I jogged down a makeshift path pushing through the stalks of corn in my way. Droplets of sweat poured down my face. Another old oak tree came into focus. I pulled myself up the rough bark and branches until I stood atop a high point. From there, I could see the familiar lights of my home and the faint shadows of our red barn.

The familiar scent of hay tingled my nose. It was coming from the left. I jumped down and ran towards the barn, wiping the tears and sweat from my face.

My legs weakened. My vision blurred. A sharp pain in my back. Blood. I collapsed onto the ground. Dirt flared up my nostrils. I gasped.

"Not today, little girl." Its ominous voice sent chills through my spine. He walked closer. "You're done. So is my job here." The scarecrow chuckled, stepped on my head, and wrenched the knife from my back. Blood dripped from my scalp along my forehead and down my cheeks. My breathing quickened. My vision blurred. I groaned, the pain piercing my back. Another chuckle. Everything went dark.

"We're just glad it's over, Jen."

I opened my eyes. Two blurry figures approached me. I blinked twice. "Lily, is that you?"

"Who else would it be?" The figure extended its glowing hand. I rubbed my eyes. Lily's transparent face came into view.

"Oh my goodness. Are you a ghost?"

126

Lily frowned at me. "What do you mean? We're all ghosts."

I glanced at the figure beside her. "Thomas, you too?"

"Speak for yourself." He pointed at me.

I looked down at my feet. They were see-through. My hands were the same. "Dammit. You're right."

Thomas laughed and intertwined his hand with Lily's. "At least we're safe now."

"No," I said, "it'll just happen again. To somebody else. The legend has to end." I walked to my friends and hugged them. Translucent tears flowed down our cheeks. Shadows melted away to reveal the house, and I caught a glimpse of the scarecrow, who stabbed my lifeless body. He kicked my head twice more before leaving.

I pushed my friends away.

Thomas pulled me back.

"I have to burn the monster's physical body," I said. "No straw can withstand fire."

Lily placed her hand on my shoulder. "We're coming with you."

Thomas stepped forward. "The three of us will stop him."

I faced the barn, and we marched ahead toward the scarecrow. "Let's do this." This time we had nothing to fear--not death, not legends, and definitely, not scarecrows.

# FRIENDSHIP GARDEN

## By Linda Lam

Friendships are flowers.
They start out as seeds,
They grow taller and taller,
But not all of them succeed.

There are blossoms and there are weeds
With toxic thorns that make you bleed.
Cut them out before they cut too deep—
What you sow is what you reap.

Sunshine is care
And water is love.
Give each flower its fair share,
And it'll bloom purely like a dove.

As time goes on, many will wilt,
But the most precious of them all will never wither.
They're not the weeds, perennials, or even the succulents,
They're the evergreens,
the ones that are there for you forever.

# BREAKING CHAINS

## By Diane Bui

Ebony shadows dance with
Autumn's last scarlet leaves.
Scarlet flames pirouette across
Midnight's dark stage.

The crackling flames engulf the
Crimson roses and yellow parchment,
Laying on a bed
Of brittle twigs.

Colors utter an ugly cry in the heat,
Of small amber tongues,
Holes widen and splinters stab,
Through the spaces of thought.

All gone as bade by the
Hand that held hand,
The mind that held memory,
The heart that held love.

# ARCHANGEL

## By Diane Bui

Sometimes I like to think to myself,
When all the world was beautiful.

It had sapphire waters and the emerald earth.
The critters were living happily and free.

The sky was clear and had
White candy floss clouds.

Stars shined brighter than the glowsticks
Around our wrists
We lived together under the constellation of fate.
Standing taller, we stood.

Buildings became our trees.
Roads, our hardened cement rivers.

Smoke conquers air, man over man.
Whatever left, waited. They waited,
For the golden gates of the heavens
To finally send its angels home.

# BURIED

## By Tuyet Duong

Didn't think I'd ever get far,
Did I even have the potential?
Didn't feel the need to try,
Why should I when I'd fail?
Didn't want others to judge me,
Could I even handle the scrutiny?

Needed others to believe in me.
How could they believe in me,
When I couldn't believe in myself?
I needed their reassurance.
Would they give it to me,
Knowing I would merely ignore them?

I lost it all in seconds.
Hopes, dreams, ambitions, purpose.
Everything good about me became replaced.
Filled with constant dread and anxiety.
When will it come tumbling down,
Until there's nothing left but pieces?

How much longer until I see,
The real girl that lies beneath?
One that still has hope,
One who spreads warmth and love,
One with light in her eyes.
The one I had buried infinitely.

# LUKE'S LITTLE ADVENTURE
## By Vicente Inciong

A NOT-SO-LONG TIME AGO, around last week, on a boring Tuesday morning, a young man was in his kitchen. But this was no ordinary young man--he was Luke Rangvaldr, the Pillar of Dawn, a knight of justice. He used the power of light to defend innocents and bring wrath upon the wicked. He had slain many enemies and protected multitudes of people. However, he was afflicted with a terrible plight.

* * *

Luke's amethyst eyes darted across the floor, searching, scouring for a sign. A clue, at least, was all he wanted. However, it was just the floor that stared back.

He lifted the refrigerator with a single hand. "No… Not there either." He dropped it down and it landed with a hard thud. With a sad look, he glanced around the kitchen once more. The brown cupboards were thrown open, the shelves pulled wide, the stove, fridge, microwave, and toaster--all moved from their original place. He slumped into a chair and ran a hand through his white hair which pointed toward the heavens, defying the grasp of gravity.

A young woman entered the kitchen. Her long auburn hair dangled down her back and her sharp emerald eyes widened in confusion.

"Luke, what did you do?"

"Hi, Jade." Luke sighed. "I was looking for something, but it isn't here."

"What were you looking for?" Jade crossed her arms.

Luke intertwined his fingers and looked away. "My keys…"

"You lost your keys? Which ones?"

*"Those keys."*

*"Those keys?"* Jade stepped back, her arms unfolded and panic washed over her.

Those keys… Luke's keys. It was extremely important that he find them again. *Without those keys--* "We must find them," she said.

"What do you think I've been trying to do?" he said. "It's not anywhere in the Citadel, that's for sure. I've searched everywhere."

"Maybe you left it somewhere else?"

"Where would I have left it? At the park?" He paused. "Actually, the park may be a very good place to start."

"You left your keys at the park?" She raised a brow, the tension dying down.

132

"Maybe. I did go there yesterday." Luke grabbed her hand and hurried out of the kitchen. "We have no time to waste. Onward." His eyes lit up and his smile widened. Maybe he'd find his keys at the park.

Jade rolled her eyes as she followed, jogging beside him, but she didn't mind coming along. She didn't have anything better to do anyway.

Halfway through their run to the park, they stopped, panting lightly.

"I didn't think this through… Let's go back and take a car," Luke said, his chest heaving. Jade nodded.

"At least we got some good cardio while it lasted," she joked as they walked back to the Citadel. They entered the base once more and got into Luke's car before driving off to the city of Rynfell.

The Citadel, their home base of operations, was far from most of the cities, but the city of Rynfell was the closest one. Luke, Jade, and the other knights and squires would normally go there if they needed to do any city-business. And besides, the park was in Rynfell anyways.

The pair reached the large and bustling city and entered its border through the main road. A clear blue sky was cast over the city, tinting massive skyscrapers of concrete and glass with a faint lavender hue. Businessmen strode down the streets talking on their phones, and women rushed across the streets to their workplace. Street performers did stunts, magic tricks, and musical numbers for passerby while stores sold goods ranging from kebabs to silk suits. Luke pulled up to the sidewalk, leaving the car by the vibrant green arch that marked the gateway into the park.

"Hopefully it's still there," he said.

"What made you lose it here anyway?" Jade looked at him with a raised brow.

"I was chased by a swarm of squirrels. It might have fallen out."

"Squirrels? Out of all the things?" Jade shook her head. "You're an idiot."

"They only attack me for some reason. Maybe because they're jealous," Luke said. He winked at her and walked into the park.

She sighed and questioned why she was following him in the first place. Then she remembered that she had nothing better to do.

The two had a peaceful walk at first, strolling past the pond where ducks ate bread crumbs that were thrown to them by other park visitors. Birds chirped a sweet and bright melody. Flowers were in bloom. All was serene and pleasant until a squirrel spotted Luke and moved after him.

Luke's blood went cold and sweat ran down his forehead. "Don't look now, but we're being followed," he whispered to Jade.

Jade turned her head to see a squirrel behind them. Her eyes widened, and she brought her hands up to her face. "Awww." She nudged Luke. "The little guy likes you."

"I told you not to look." Luke began walking faster and kept his eyes on the squirrel. It looked like he was about to win a walkathon championship title.

The squirrel dashed after him, running past Jade and latching onto his leg with its claws and teeth.

Luke screeched and charged ahead with his arms flailing in the air. Three more squirrels lunged out from trees and bushes, all latching onto him as he fled.

All Jade could see now was Luke running off into the distance, covered in brown rodents. She face-palmed. "Time to go save him… I guess…"

After an hour of chasing after Luke and fighting off squirrels, the two sat down on a park bench. Luke was covered in light bite marks and fur, his hair was a mess, and he kept flashing looks at the trees.

Jade patted his back. "There, there, Luke. No one else saw you shriek and run off like a spaghetti monster." She chuckled and nudged him on the shoulder.

Luke shivered, shaking his head and ruffling his hair to get some of the brown fur out. "No one can ever know about this." He took in a deep breath. "It's bad for my rep."

Jade's smile grew. "It's delicious blackmail for the future."

A woman's scream came out from the distance, catching both of their attention. Luke stood up and shook the fur off his body.

He nodded to Jade and the two dashed over to the source of the scream. In a clearing, a masked man with a knife stood over a woman, poking his victim in the side with the blade. He was large and burly, and his voice sounded like gravel.

"Cough it up, lady. It's your wallet or your gu--" The man was interrupted by a hard, metal fist pounding into the side of his face. A loud crash resonated through the park as Luke, now in his full suit of black, metallic armor, sent the robber flying into a nearby tree. "Leave her alone," Luke said. He stood over the man with his fists clenched and faint golden light gleaming off his suit. "If there's one thing I hate more than squirrels, it's scumbags like you who think they can just pull off stunts like this."

The robber curled into a ball and whimpered in response.

The woman ran toward him, wrapping her arms around his torso. She smiled up at Luke with glistening eyes. "Thank you. If it weren't for--"

"Thanks can come later. You should go get the police," Luke said, patting her on the shoulder.

Jade crossed her arms and watched Luke's demeanor change from a fearsome Knight to a caring savior. Her eyes narrowed, but for a different reason.

134

"I-I will. Thank you." The woman turned to run, but was cut off by Jade.

"Hang on," Jade said, holding out an arm out toward the woman. "What did you place on him?"

Luke collapsed onto one knee; green smoke oozed out of the gaps in his armor and helmet. He coughed and gagged, his chest heaving, gasping for air. His strength was fading; he couldn't keep his fist clenched. The thug from the tree nearby walked over and slammed a large branch into Luke's side, sending him into another tree.

The woman smirked at Jade. "You two are such idiots... Roaming around here without any security." She unsheathed a hidden dagger from her garments and thrust it at Jade.

Jade dodged the blade, then grabbed her wrist and crushed it, the bones grinding into dust within her grasp. The woman shrieked and fell to her knees. Jade's eyes glowed bright emerald and her voice rang through the trees.

"You may have gotten the Knight, but you forgot about me."

The thug stepped back, holding his branch tighter. "You're his squire? We thought you were just some lover girl her was dragging along."

Jade twisted the woman's wrist, forcing another scream out of the assassin. "Lover girl? Looks like I fooled you." She smirked. "I didn't even try." She threw the woman straight at the thug, sending them both flying against another tree. Both the dagger and branch flew out of their hands.

She moved over to Luke and knelt down, examining his armor.

"Still awake, I see." She peered into his suit and pulled out a device that was stuck between the armor plates. It was a small mechanism that was designed to release a poisonous gas that inhibited a Pillar's ability to utilize his superhuman traits. This poison was designed to take down Knights like Luke. She took it between two fingers and crushed it, and the green smoke stopped pouring out from Luke's armor. Moments later, he gasped for air and was able to breathe again.

Luke groaned and stood up. "That was embarrassing. All I wanted to do was find my keys." Both of them walked over to the groaning assassins and loomed over them.

"So, you two are assassins, eh?" Luke asked, crossing his arms.

The two looked up at him. "Long live Barnathos."

He flinched at the sound of that name, the name of a terrorist leader.

"Gross." He looked over at Jade, smirking at her. "I suppose this is a good way to relieve stress."

"Especially after being chased by squirrels."

"Shut up." Luke slammed his fist into his palm. He cracked his knuckles and the two below him whimpered. "Now... I've had a less than remarkable day today. I lost my keys, ran for no good reason, got chased by a swarm of killer rats-with-tails..." His eyes flashed a powerful golden light. "And now I have two idiots trying to kill me." He raised his fist and Jade followed, raising her own fist.

She smirked and her eyes glowed green again. "We're going to show you exactly what happens when you mess with us on a bad day."

Luke and Jade punched the assassins, hearing the satisfying crunch of teeth getting knocked out of their mouths. Another punch to the stomach, another to the ribs, to the diaphragm, to the neck, to the collar, to the nose, and repeat. Their fists turned into a flurry of emerald and golden light, streaking off the bodies of their human punching bags. Both Luke and Jade roared with intense fury as they unleashed barrages of punches on the two hapless terrorists.

"This'll teach you--" They both delivered uppercuts to their respective dummies, sending them flying into the air before jumping up to meet them.

"To never mess with us again." They slammed their fists into their faces, sending the two straight down to the ground.

Luke and Jade both landed by the unconscious bodies. Jade sighed and pulled out her phone to call the police. Her glowing eyes faded back to normal.

Luke stared at the two, his eyes locked on their broken faces, the golden aura and glow around his armor and eyes dissipating. His breathing slowed and calmed; the rage within him died down.

Hours later, he sat down on a park bench a mile away from the scene. Jade sat next to him, keeping some distance between them at first. Her eyes scanned him. He was still in his armor, holding his hands together and staring straight at the ground. Luke was always like this, always brooding after a fight with terrorists.

She sighed and scooted closer. "Let me guess. You feel guilty."

He turned his head and looked up at her, his brows furrowed. He said nothing and looked away at the ground.

"It isn't your fault that this happens, you know?"

Luke sighed. "I know. Doesn't make me feel any better."

"Then what will?"

His head tilted to look toward her feet, his eyes still locked on the ground.

"You can't keep saying that you know but still act like you blame yourself." She scooted closer. She had been through this a couple of times with him, helping him through his self-punishing thoughts after fights, so she decided to change her approach. A small smile came to her face and her eyes became gentle. She glanced down to his locked hands. "Remember when that grandma offered to give you dinner after you saved her eight-hundred year old cat from a tree?"

He chuckled for a brief moment, shaking his head. "I still don't understand how a cat that old got up there in the first place."

"Or when you saved a farm from a dragon attack? That was fun, right?" Jade put a hand over his. They loosened at her touch.

"I guess...yeah."

"They even offered you two buckets of milk."

He looked up at her now, chuckling. "And instead of refusing politely, I asked if it was pasteurized."

"You're such a doofus. And people love you for it." She nudged his shoulder. "My point is that there will be people who disagree with you. People want to challenge the Pillars. There will be the terrorists of Barnathos."

Luke nodded, glancing away for a moment. He turned his head to look at the ground again, but she placed a hand on the side of his helmet and brought his face back to look at her. His eyes locked with hers now.

"But you can't forget everyone else. You can't forget about the people that support you, that appreciate you." She smiled. "The people that love you."

He smiled too, a genuine smile that grew across his face.

"You are the Pillar of Dawn, the Knight of Light, the chosen warrior of the goddesses before they left this world. They, and all the other people of this world, trust you and the other Pillars to protect us." She put her head on his shoulder, gripping his hands tighter.

His two joined hands parted, one of them taking her hand. His armor faded, de-summoning itself.

"Don't lose faith in yourself. Not while everyone else still has faith in you." She whispered. "People believe in you, Luke." She stroked her thumb over the back of his hand. "I believe in you."

He softened and slumped closer to her. "Thank you, Jade," He said. "I knew I made the right choice by recruiting you as my squire."

"Yeah, well." She leaned her head against his. "Don't get used to it. You'd be a helpless, sobbing mess without me." She nudged his shoulder and giggled.

Luke scoffed, shaking his head. "I suppose you're right. For now."

They stayed on that bench for a half-hour, watching the birds sing before deciding to leave.

As he stood up, he heard a familiar jingle.

"Wait a second--"

He shook his hips to the sides, back and forth, swinging an invisible hula hoop around his waist. The jingling got louder.

"WAIT A SECOND--"

She threw her head back and groaned. "You're kidding me, right?"

137

Luke reached into his pockets. The two front ones, empty. He reached back and put his hand into his back-left pocket. Cold metal poked his fingers. He grabbed it, yanking out his keys.

"They were in my pocket?" He blinked a few times, and shook his head.

Jade face-palmed and groaned again.

"Huh…Weird." He placed them back into his pocket and scratched his head. "How did it get in there?"

Jade sighed and threw her arms around Luke's neck, giving him a warm hug. "You're such an idiot, you know that?"

He just stared straight ahead, trying to process everything that happened, trying to understand why his keys were there.

Jade smirked, proud that she had successfully slipped the keys back into Luke's pocket while he was brooding from the fight. Why did she keep the keys for the entire time you ask?

We may never know.

# HUMAN SACRIFICE

## By Monica Van

Fires of Hell burn bright
On Earth.
For the cruelty of humans is
Second to none.
Rituals glorify
The sanctity of customs,
But conformity undermines
The sanctity of life.
Death rituals glorify
The beasts of myth and divinity
But humans are the true beasts
On Earth,
For only they can harness
The fires of Hell.

# AVOCADO

## By Alex Quang

what used to be just a cup of coffee
is now a way to wake up my morning to the thought  of you

a sweater i threw on casually before
is now a reminder of the nights it's gone unwashed to preserve your smell

and the garden with moist brown soil and vibrant colors of unimaginable art
is now a canvas of your eyes and your soul

and now i realize i don't only see the world differently since meeting you

im seeing love the way you taught me to

# DREAMS

## By Aamir Yusuf

The dream I chase is wonderful,
I risk everything for this dream,
Going to the place where it exists,
Working hard, taking no breaks,
Hoping that one day this dream will come true.
Pursuing this dream till the end or till it happens,
Being with the people I achieved this dream with,
Or being alone without the people I dream of being with,
Rejected but never failing,
To fail will be to die,
But at least I'll know I tried,
Giving up won't settle these feelings,
Because my heart and mind will just keep dreaming.

# DONE WITH LOVE

Based on the painting "What Is Done with Love Is Done Well" by Vincent Van
Gogh

**By Katie Luong**

With shaken legs and a thumping heart
I wanted you in my arms and by my side,
But what I didn't expected was that you
Were to be my last and only love.

I held onto the black box in my coat pocket
While you walked silently beside me
With a gloomy look in your eyes,
I asked you, "What's wrong?"
But I will never know.

You began to tear up before you stopped
Midway down the wet, glossy sidewalk.
I watched you try to gather your
Scrambled thoughts, as if you were denying
A crime that you never committed.

On one knee, I bent before you and
Raised the open black box to your teary eyes
"I love you. I want to spend the rest of my life with you.
Will you marry me?"
I closed my eyes, awaiting the words.

"I can't. I'm sorry."
With that, I lost faith in finding someone.
No matter how long my friends and family
Keep telling me to move on,
I will never find love again.

# YOU

## By Mikayla Reilly

Your laugh was the first thing I noticed,
Drawing me in like a kid to a candy shop.
I couldn't stop staring at your eyes,
They were as blue as the ocean.
Your smile was contagious,
I couldn't help but mimic.

I was captivated.
You were my everything,
And I didn't want you to leave.
I had finally found a reason to be happy:
You.

This poem, I dedicate it to you.
My knight in shining armor,
Who saved me from the pits of hell,
And showed me the light of a new world,

A world in which I could
Live,
Trust,
And love again.

# THE REBELLION

## By April Thong

IT WAS A FINE spring morning on the walk to school. Looking up at the blue sky, I couldn't help but feel absolute bliss. The whole world, illuminated by sparkling dewdrops, was soaked in the sun's glory. The perfume of newly blossomed flowers mixed with the crisp air, creating an intoxicating aroma. The chilly temperature gently nudged adolescents closer to one another, each brush of the hands resulting in apple red cheeks. In that moment, they believed in love. The gentle hums of nearby bees harmonized with the birds' sweet melody. This was the very essence of life itself. Naturally, we all waltzed through the gates in a trance, drunk from the spring air.

Then the bell rang and all dreams came to an end.

Over the speaker, the Voice issued a single command. "Teachers, please close your doors. This is a tardy sweep. Thank you."

We all snapped back to reality after hearing this familiar, yet deadly phrase. Here, at La Quinta High School, there has been a strong focus on character building, namely punctuality. At random, the Voice would proclaim this line, causing late students to be brutally beaten and hauled off to their doom. Whether it is due to your car breaking down and having to run to school or a sibling taking too long to get ready as you wait for the restroom, it all results in the same, sad fate. So far, no one has been able to escape.

*One, two, three, four. One, two, three, four.* Admins in armor came marching out with weapons at their sides; the rhythmic steps growing increasingly loud as they poured out of every possible entrance. Classroom doors were slammed shut in one thunderous clap. It had begun. All around students scrambled like cockroaches, searching for safety. There were snot, tears, and prayers. I dashed into the nearest building and hid behind the door. Crouching, I peered through the glass partition to examine the situation at hand.

Black padded creatures pounced on unsuspecting students, whose bodies dropped to the ground as they made contact with Taser guns. As I scanned the area, I accidentally made eye contact with one of the admins. *Ba-dum. Ba-dum.* The speed of my heart rate picked up as beads of sweat gathered on my palms after I realized my mistake. I jumped up and sprinted down the halls, feeling the ever

144

growing presence of the enemy behind me, with no plan in mind but the will to survive, I turned the corner and saw a light in the distance. I halted abruptly, thinking through my options. One, get caught and thrashed about mercilessly. Two, forgo all suspicion and hope that this light was not a trap. Not having much of a choice, I chose the latter.

The light led me deeper and deeper into the building. Darkness began to close in on me, but thankfully the light stopped and soon I caught up with it. There stood a small, poised woman with golden hair. Her gentle and kind smile was not to be mistaken as meekness for there was something fierce about her. Perhaps it was the way she carried herself with her head held high and her shoulders never once slouching. She ushered me to follow her into a room. I entered and found myself in a place, where despite its location in the heart of immense darkness, natural light poured in through sunroofs. Ancient books lined the walls from top to bottom and various plants sat around, their green, twisting arms stretching as far as possible. In the woman's hands was a book with an image of a roaring lion engraved on the cover.

"Hello, Kira. It's nice to finally meet you," the woman said from behind me. My eyes widened as I realized I hadn't introduced myself. The little woman laughed at my confusion. "Ever since the school's tardy policy changed, I've been searching for a student who would restore this place to its former glory. That's how I came to learn about you." Her brows furrowed. "It's a shame how they treat students nowadays."

"A student? Restore this place to its former glory?" I opened my mouth in disbelief. "Me?"

"Yes, you. You are the one that's destined to save us from the tyrannical admins," she exclaimed.

I was speechless. The very idea of me, Kira Park, changing the system, was mind-boggling. I was not an active participant in any school events, sports, or clubs. I didn't even have grades. I had always been that average student who never drew attention to myself and now I was told that I would make history.

"Of course, I will provide items to aid you for the journey," she reassured me.

She guided me to a wooden chest against the furthest wall. From it, the woman pulled out a rolled-up scroll, a lantern, and a dark brown cloak before handing them to me. I opened the scroll. Painted onto the ancient paper was a layout of the school, the same map that was on the back of the school agenda. I looked at the woman and was about to tell her that this map was completely unnecessary when she took it and stretched it to an even greater length. A blueprint of all sorts of secret tunnels and hidden rooms were sketched out. *Wow*, I mouthed as she smiled at me. Next, I analyzed the lantern. Peering inside, all I could see was one strand of golden hair. The woman recognized my puzzled look and without saying anything, she covered the sunroofs. Frightened by the sudden darkness, I whipped around trying to find the woman while jostling the lantern. The strand of hair instantly lit up and it was no longer dark. This was the same light I had followed earlier. Lastly, with the sunroofs uncovered once again, she fastened the cloak around my neck. Because of its bulky metal frame, I was surprised to find it weightless as it adjusted accordingly to the temperature, keeping me warm.

"In order to restore La Quinta to its former glory, you must defeat the Voice," whispered the little woman in urgency. I nodded in full acceptance. She took a deep breath and roared, flinging open the door with its force. "Now, go!" she commanded and the room disappeared, leaving me alone in the darkness. I shook the lantern. The light revealed a narrow passageway leading to who-knows-where. I opened my map and followed the path that would lead me to the Voice.

Upon venturing, I caught sight of a moving torch in the distance. I scrambled towards the closest hiding spot, an indent in the wall. I pressed my back against the cold, stony structure and turned off my lantern. With each stride, the person got closer. I held my breath when the light was only a foot away. Squeezing my eyes shut, I prayed that whoever it was would pass by oblivious to me hiding. Light shined against my eyelids. I looked. The torch was inches away from my face allowing me only to see a pair of thick frames.

"What are you doing?" His booming voice echoed. This time, he moved further away. There he stood in the flickering light in an all too familiar suit. Black padding covered his entire body. However, his head remained uncovered for his helmet was at his side. The logo on his chest only confirmed my fear; he was an admin. The man shifted his gaze from me, to my map, and then my cloak. He then noticed the lantern at my side and snatched it up. With his torch at the mouth of my lantern, he peered inside. Looking back at me he whispered, "You're the One." His expression was difficult to read. Fearful, I groped around for any nearby weapons. Satisfied with a potato-sized rock, I gripped it in my hands.

"Oh, don't worry," he reassured me. "I'm part of the rebellion." He took out a book, identical to the one the tiny woman had in her hands, for proof before handing me back my lantern. "Just be careful. These halls are used by admins and rebels alike." As we said our goodbyes, there seemed to be a change in his expression. For a moment, it seemed as if his lips had been twisted up into a sinister smile, but after glancing again, only the same solemn lines were present. Thus, I left in a hurry with the rock still in my hands.

I travelled down deeper into the school when I heard laughter coming from behind a closed door. Curious, I decided to go in. Upon entering, I was greeted by a most spectacular sight. There sat a girl with curly hair, each strand seemingly running off in all sorts of different directions. A second girl had a bowl shaped haircut. As for the boy, he stood there shoving pizza down his throat. Every time he laughed, pieces of food flew out of the boy's mouth making them giggle even harder. A disco ball scattered various colors of lights across the room. Plaster on the walls was humorous, satirical pictures labeled under "Best Memes." Light was supplied by an enormous computer screen that took up one side of the room from top to bottom. On it, they played Shooting Stars by Bag Raiders.

I took a step further into the room. *Crunch*. Both music and laughter stopped as everyone whipped around to eye the intruder. Under my foot were the remains of what used to be a chip. The boy's jaw dropped open; mashed up food on full display. The girl's already frazzled hair was on ends now. As for the other girl, she clasped her hands together joyfully. In a hurry, they pushed, pulled, and tugged me towards the computer, obviously excited to show me something. After a series of passwords and security questions, a page popped up revealing propaganda against tardy sweeps. They looked at me eagerly. A smile broke across my face knowing that I was not alone in this fight. However, time was ticking and I still had a long ways to go. With newfound motivation, I continued my journey.

I walked along the dark and damp pathway. Strange shadows danced around me, but their owners were never to be seen. The sound of water dripping from the rocks intensified due to the structure of the area, causing me to jump with fright. The closer I got to the Voice, the more eerie my surroundings became. I turned the corner. There, standing in front of the path was an army of admins. Leading them was the man who held his helmet at his side. His eyes looked at me in amusement behind its thick lens.

"Did you really think you could stop me?" He laughed, the sound echoing through the tunnels. "No one has ever been able to escape the sweeps."

"You're the Voice," I whispered, shocked from the revelation.

He chuckled. "It took you long enough to find out." His laughter ceased as the once solemn expression took its spot. "You don't know how long I've waited for this day to come. To defeat you and reign over this school forever, it'd be a dream come true." He tossed a book to the ground. Although it was battered and torn, I could see by the seal on its cover that it was the same one he had shown me earlier. "Of course, I had to first get rid of that midget of a woman. Funny how I met you right after I had my little appointment with her. Oh, and let's not forget about Moe, Larry, and Curly." The smirk on his face sickened me.

"Where are they?" I screamed. Anger spread through my body as I thought of the tiny woman and the trio being beaten and bruised by those filthy admins. With the same potato-sized rock in my hand, I ran towards him, ready to smash his head in.

"Seize her!" he yelled. There was a scuffle as I tried to fight them off. Just then, I saw my chance to put an end to the Voice when I felt the impact of something heavy against my head. Warm liquid oozed down and I reached up to touch it. Looking back at my hand, I saw that it was covered in red. Then, everything went black.

# THE ABYSS

## By Bryan Le

There is something amiss
Here in this abyss
Instead of wind and silence
There are sounds of screams and violence
Somewhere in this abyss
You can hear a hiss
As worshippers place bodies at the steps
The hissing begins to grow
Oh, the slitherer is on the go
Those who haven't been sacrificed
Have started to pray for their life through Christ
But hoping mercy shall be upon them,
They have become numb
Tears start to form, as you hear their prayers
Because there's nothing that can end their despair
There is nothing you can do against the malicious deity
All you can do is pity
"Those be pray to me from earth, believing I still reside in heaven,"
"I have reincarnated, but right now, I am only human, please, let me be forgiven."
"I hear words of another deity here, is it Christ, the son of God?"
"Oh this what I am supposed to do with the song of God;
Oh, this is quite odd."
Christ, the son of God, does not know fear, but as of right now, he is no longer
here.
He has become disheartened.
Christ, the son of god, is now to be sacrificed to the malicious being.
Now, there is no more fleeing.
The story is over, the darkness has devoured the earth
Now it is only a planet with no worth.

# STRONG-WILLED

## By Cheyenne Danielle Hunt

Snow highlights her eyes, her cheeks, her smiles
Showing the innocence of her as a child
Smiling and running with cheer and pride

Surfing with her best friend by her side
She shines with the water of the ocean
They smile and laugh--best friends for life

Riding away on her horse in the countryside
She is the champion--the happiest girl alive
She shines, laughs, and smiles

But on that Christmas morning
--No longer the happiest girl alive--
She lost her best friend in life

She becomes a different girl
Who cannot control her pain
Lashing out at others in vain

Those who don't understand pick on her
Those who can't feel for her pain fight her
Those who don't understand will mock her

Her dreams become nightmares
Her nightmares become reality
Numb for a year--her heart turned cold.

Her father, proud of her, tells her,
"You have a kind heart, social butterfly, and
no matter what you'll always be my baby girl."

Pushing forward--she is a fighter
Finding happiness on her own
Won't let anyone bring her down.

Thank you, Dad, with your love
Smiling and laughing again,
I am strong-willed.

# PRESSURE
## By Kristy Diep

Most days,
The pressure was heavier than others,
I found it hard to breath,
The wind from my lungs,
Stripped.
I gasped short intakes of nitrogen,
For oxygen was far too extinct
From the reality that held me still.

Other days,
It was a softer,
Lighter ton of steel,
Large tides crashed in at the peak of sunset,
And I stood,

I stood,
Allowed the waves to beat me down,
And pull me into the abyss of the sea,
As I met a cold embrace,
Engulfed under the surface of the visible eye,
Lost.

The water sank into my organs,
It floated around
And mixed what wasn't meant to be combined,
And I, I was rearranged into the wrong order.

These days,
I try,
I paint the flowers yellow,
Sprinkle my cupcakes with rainbows,
Tug smiles on faces,

Pump blood into hearts,
And pour
Pour the water out of the ocean,
Keep it in dams,
So that others,
Don't have to feel the pressure.

# POURING RAIN

### By Kenna B. James

The rain keeps falling,
Falling,
Thunder.
Lightning.
Hail.
When will it stop?
Nobody knows.
Will it ever stop?
Raining buckets,
Flooded,
Unsafe to drive,
What goes up
Must always come down.
Raining,
Pouring,
When it will stop,
Nobody knows.
Rain.
Tears.
Thunder.
Lightning.
Fears.
Hail.
Wind.
What's happening?
When will it end?

# SONNET V

## By Thong Pham

With fleeting thoughts I swore a vow
And crossed my heart upon the moon
To languished Love I'd never bow
Over beauty and song, to never swoon

But with sweet melody and playful flirt
Tempered so with gentle caress
Wounded pride cannot further be hurt
For broken is my oath, I shall confess

For falling is the natural state
So begone this fear and delusion
With clarity, an acceptance of fate
To cast away this ill-conceived illusion

My luck demands to take a chance
With this twirling whirlwind romance

# THE FINAL HIKE

## By Jennifer Chau

"JESUS, PENN. ARE YOU breaking already?" Dave asked.

"I'm fine." Truth was, I broke twenty minutes ago. My arms dangled like broken limbs by my sides.

"Great," Dave said, "because we still have another two miles before the real hike actually starts."

I groaned.

"We should do this more often." Holly batted her eyes at Troy.

Troy smiled. "Sure. We're all friends."

I glanced at Dave who shrugged. We laughed then it was silent except for the crunch of leaves under our feet.

Holly sped up to walk ahead of us. "You know," she said, her voice growing soft. "People say this trail is haunted."

"Why are we even here then?" I asked.

Dave leaned into my ear and whispered, "To sacrifice Holly."

"If anyone's going to end up dead, it's me," I said. "Remember what happened last year?"

"Last Halloween?"

"Yes, it was twelve A.M. You guys left me outside, alone, in the dark while you shoved each other into the door of the haunted house, screaming and laughing."

Dave shook his head. "Sometimes, I wonder how you still put up with us."

We crossed along a path sheltered by tall sycamore trees towering over us. Sunlight glistened through the leaves in golden rays, and every now and again a soft breeze blew through and invigorated us. A squirrel jumped onto the path out of nowhere, took a look at us invading its territory, and jumped back into the wilderness, its tail fluttering behind it like a puff of cotton.

Dewdrops dripped from the leaves and blades of grass tickled our ankles while we walked through patches of greenery. I breathed in the fresh smell of moss and trees, which brought back childhood memories of running through fields and streams.

A peacock appeared and Troy, stupid and reckless as usual, thought it was a good idea to tug on one of its feathers. The fowl made a horrible shriek and yanked on Troy's shirt. Then it receded into the woods while Holly, Dave, and I laughed like hysterical monsters.

After another twenty minutes, my legs were on the verge of collapse. We paused at the entrance of the trail.

"Let's take a break." I took a big gulp of water from my flask.

"No, way." Holly kept walking. Troy and Dave followed Holly on the trail. I scowled and jogged to catch up.

"How are you not tired?" I asked.

"Like we've said before, you need more exercise." Holly chuckled and lowered her voice, "I heard some people don't even make it out alive. A secret cult meets here every Sunday night. Well, at least that's what people say. Sunday is supposed to be the holy day, so they gather around there in a circle and summon the devil to come and play. Apparently, spirits wander in the forest." She looked at us with wide eyes and added, "Some people even get possessed."

We dismissed her wild stories and kept hiking along a stream that led up to the top of the hill. Water trickled down layers of pebbles as the sound of the flowing current filled our ears. The water splashed against my ankles, the coolness of the water energizing me.

The others began to leave me behind. "Slow down, guys," I said. Somehow they had sprinted through the path and hoisted themselves up boulders and past large streams as if it was a mild walk through the park. Meanwhile, my eyes were fixed on the ground. Step here, not there, and avoid the poison ivy.

"Hurry up, Penn!" Dave shouted.

Still falling behind, I followed them up a steep hill that seemed to stretch on forever. Thick brushes grew on both sides, leaves were scattered everywhere. The rocks beneath my feet were loose, causing me to slip almost every other step. By the middle half of the trudge, I was on all fours. My knees were caked in mud, my palms scratched like leather, and my mind felt lost.

"I'm feeling sick, guys." I groaned. By the time we were at the top of the hill, I was already flat on the ground. I felt nauseated.

"Fine. We'll take a break," Holly said. She stopped by a big tree and leaned against it. Troy collapsed onto the ground beside her.

"I'm feeling light-headed. Is anyone else?" Dave asked. He put his hands to his face and exhaled. "You doing okay, Penn?"

"Barely," I whispered. "Are we almost at the peak?"

"I don't know," Holly said. "But we can't turn around now."

"I'm feeling really sick and I've gone on worse hikes than this," Dave said. "This isn't normal."

"Could it be something we ate?" I asked.

"We didn't even eat breakfast together," Dave said, wiping off the sweat on his forehead with a sleeve. "It couldn't be."

"Uuuhhh," Troy moaned.

"You all right?" Dave asked. He tossed Troy his flask. "Drink up, dude."

The flask flew across the air and bounced off Troy's leg. "Uuuhhh," he moaned again. He closed his eyes and let his head topple from side to side.

Holly put her hands on his shoulder and shook him gently. "What's wrong? Are you feeling sick? Say something."

"Give him the water," Dave said.

Holly grabbed the flask and untwisted the cap. "Open up, Troy," she said, putting it to his mouth.

"Uuuhhh." Troy kept shaking his head, and his mouth gaped open.

"Troy?" Holly tipped the flask sideways and let some water flow into his mouth. "Guys, I'm going to find some help. I think I saw a cabin someway back there. You guys stay with Troy, okay? Don't let him go anywhere."

"Are you sure you want to go alone? I can go with you," I said, standing up.

"It's okay. I'm fine going alone." Holly turned back. "You'll just slow me down anyways."

"What's that supposed to mean?" I grabbed her shoulder, but she shook it off. She jogged down the path until she was beyond our view.

"Don't let her get to you," Dave said. "She's just flustered because of him." He pointed at Troy who continued moaning. "To be honest, I think she sort of likes him."

"I guess," I said, shrugging. "She's right though. I don't even know why I'm here with you guys today. I don't usually come anyways."

"Nah, Penn, don't say that. It's been really fun with you here. It's funny teasing you, too." Dave said.

"Stop." I nudged him with my arm.

Troy began laughing hysterically. "I've won, guys." He began cackling now, and his eyes were bloodshot.

Dave took a step forward. "Are you alright, Troy?"

Troy's face was red, and he was still cackling. Dave put his hands on Troy's shoulders to calm him down, but it was no use.

"Troy, what's wrong?" I asked. I bent down in front of him and whispered, "Are you okay?"

"Die," Troy said. He laughed at the word. "Die, die, die."

I jumped away from him. "Dave, why is he saying that? What's happening to him?" A cold sweat ran down my face. "This isn't Troy. Troy isn't like this."

"I don't understand," Dave whispered.

Troy leapt off the ground onto his feet and ran to the edge of the cliff. He faced the edge and spread his arms out wide.

"Troy!" I shouted.

Dave grabbed onto his arm. "You're going to fall off."

I held onto Troy's other arm.

Troy only laughed. "Fall off? And what, die?" He looked at us with a deranged smile. "I've already won."

He yanked his arm away and jumped.

Time seemed to freeze. My ears rang.

* * *

"What the hell is going on, Dave?" I was crying. "And where is Holly?"

"I don't know what's going on. He's not down there either," Dave said. There were tears in his eyes.

"What do you mean he's not down there?" I walked toward the edge and looked down.

"I don't see his body."

The brush behind us rustled. I froze.

Dave looked at me. "Who's there?"

No answer.

I leaned on his arm and whispered, "Do you think we're being watched?"

"I don't know," he said, his voice trembling. He grabbed my hand and pulled me closer. "Don't leave my side."

"What do we do now?"

"We need to look for Holly."

We hiked back down the hill and along the path toward the cabin. We didn't see any sign of Troy's body anywhere. The hike was deathly silent. We passed through the same brushes and streams. Every shadow seemed to jump out at us. I was—no—we were scared.

"This trail is haunted," I said. "I want to go home."

A high pitched scream rang through the dense trees.

"Holly?" Dave called.

"The voice came from that direction." I pointed. We ran into a dense section of trees and brushes. Sharp bristles scratched my ankles and all along my arm, but I didn't care. The closer we got, the louder the voice became, and we realized that there was more than one voice. In fact, there were probably at least twenty.

159

A large group of people were congregated in a large circle, chanting the same lines over and over again, but I couldn't make out what was being said. Die? Spirits?

"It's the cult," Dave said.

"Don't be too loud," I whispered. "I don't want them to know we're here."

"Can you see what's going on?"

The group was composed of men and women, from their early twenties to late forties. They were all encircled around something in the center.

"I can't tell what they're congregating around." I craned my neck to see. A young man, presumably in his mid-twenties, was standing in an inner circle. He wore a large, black robe, and he was holding a large torch. He was leading the chants, swaying back and forth to the rhythm.

"Come over to where I'm standing. I can lift you up," Dave said. He held onto my waist and hoisted me up from the ground.

I squinted toward the middle. "It looks like a wooden contraption, and there's someone's in the center."

The man finally moved.

"It's Holly."

The group stood around a large, wooden three-holed structure that entrapped Holly's head and hands. Her cheek was bleeding.

"Holly?" Dave asked.

"She's captured. We have to save her, Dave. They've put her in a wooden stock."

"A stock? What is this, the Medieval Age?"

"Apparently." I stretched my head further to get a clearer glimpse of everything going on. The cult was still chanting something. "Poor Holly... We have to do something. They're shaming her, and..." My voice trailed off.

"And what?" Dave asked, impatient.

"There's something on the ground," I said, squinting. "Something big..."

"What?" Dave asked. "What is it?"

"It's a body. Brown hair, I think, and... freckles all over the face."

"No," Dave said. He almost threw me on the ground. "It's not—"

"—Troy," I said. I almost cried as the name escaped my lips. "I think he's dead."

"No!" Dave shouted.

"Don't scream, Dave," I said. My voice trembled. "They'll hear us."

It was too late.

The chanting stopped, and all heads turned toward where we were standing. The man in the black robe pointed at us with his finger and shouted, "Intruders."

All at once, the mob of angry cult members ran toward us.

"Run!" I sprinted back into the woods, my legs scrambling over branches and puddles on the ground. The mud sloshed around my ankles. My heart was pounding. "Dave!" I shouted. But there was no answer. I didn't hear any more footsteps running. I stopped running and looked around--Dave was gone.

"No, no, no…" I whispered. I stopped at a tree and crouched onto the ground. "Holly's captured, Troy's dead, and Dave's missing." Tears welled up in my eyes. "I can't do this alone. I can't do this alone."

That was when I saw the smoke. Black ash stifling the air. It got hot, really hot, and I realized:

The cult had lit the forest on fire.

I picked myself up off the ground and ran. I didn't look back once.

* * *

"I'm sorry about what I said earlier. Obviously. You're the one who saved us all," Holly said. Her clothes were covered in dirt, and her cheek was bandaged.

"All I did was slow us down, remember?"

"No, I'm sorry I said that. Thank God you called the police about this. They found Dave, and guess what? Apparently the cult had been smuggling and burning illegal drugs on these mountain trails. The toxic fumes caused us to hallucinate." Holly sobbed.

Dave sat in a stunned silence twenty feet away surrounded by a paramedic and two police officers.

"Girls," an officer approached us. He had a grim look on his face. "We believe we've found Troy's body. We need you to confirm the identity."

I cried. "So it's true. He really is dead. I had somehow hoped it had all been a bad dream."

# THICK CAT NAMED CHUNK

Based on the painting Still Life with Green Soup (Fernando Botero; 1972)

**By Maggie Tieu**

The neighbors claim I am lonely
Others say I thought him up
because I crave attention
Regardless, he still comes every night

An unholy being peels
out of the shadows of my home
Prowls into the room
Hunting predator eyes

Interrupting a quiet dinner with
Me and my reflection on the wall
Replacing my midnight meal
With what most would call--
Tasteless garbage

But He doesn't care
He jesters with his stiff inhuman limbs
Eat, he tells me
Every night
Every meal
No other voice but his deep bellow
Eat, he says
Over
And over again
Just
Eat.

# HOT WINTER NIGHTS
## By Kristy Diep

Break a sweat, and it'll trickle down your spine,
Becoming the dew that early mornings bring upon us,
Mixing our essence of expression and passion
Into poison.

The warm breeze blows, sending chills down our paintings,
Forms of literary pictures that never seem to be complete.

He who seeks to find what is missing
Is bound to appreciate what he has,
Not understanding contentment is just a childhood issue
That crawled under depths, rising above into adulthood,
Falling right side up into the vastness of ending possibilities.

Ice cold water pours over and kills the overheating engine,
From which the smoke of the innocent evaporates into the velvet sheet draped
over the living.

As the night falls,
Boiling water pours onto the snow,
Turning our warm hearts cold,
And war,
The weapons that mold into words that kill more than those
Being born,
Is forgotten simply.

And on those hot winter nights,
We oppose those who don't agree.

# DEEP BREATHS

## By Gabrielle Romero

As you wrap your hands around my throat,
I look you in the eyes,
Searching for any sign of remorse,
A remnant of who you used to be,
Someone I know you could be.

With each finger surely leaving its mark,
Breathing--no longer as easy as it once seemed,
But I let you squeeze tighter,

Because how dare I breathe
Without your permission.
I apologize for the inconvenience.

I soothe your hands,
And tell you: *it's going to be all right,*

As if you're the one who needs convincing.

# WHERE I AM FROM...

## By Kenna B. James

I am from a two story house,
I am from the dining room behind the bar chairs,
Where I can see the grapefruit tree from the window,
Whose long gone limbs I remember as if they were my own.

I am from Mom and Dad's Christian faith,
Where our annual ornament exchange parties
Were the talk of the neighborhood.

I am from good mornings with fresh pancakes,
Eating lunch at Islands, drinking their sweet strawberry
milkshakes,
To long nights watching Wipeout and AFV,
And sleepovers with Grandma and Grandpa.

I am from bedtime stories,
"Goodnight Swamp Rat" to "Good morning Merry Sunshine"
And sleepless Fourth of July nights
With family fun and homemade ice cream.

This is where I am from,
And I am proud.

# THE LOVE THAT NEVER LASTS

## By Mikayla Reilly

I noticed you from across the street,
Your back towards me.
Head tilted, your laughter filling the air
Bringing a little more joy into this cold world.
The skin around your beautiful gray blue eyes crinkle,
Full pink lips pull up toward rosy cheeks,
Wavy brown hair dancing in the wind.
Naming only a few of the reasons why,
I fell in love with you.

We were perfect together,
The golden boy with the golden girl,
You were the prince, and I the princess.
Everyone knew we were meant to be.
Nothing could tear us apart.
We would last, I'd say,
Together forever, you'd tell me.

You'd show up out of the blue some days,
Asking me, begging for forgiveness
And I'd always say yes.
I never did know what you were sorry for.
It couldn't have been that bad.
Because you always came back.

But you'd come back drunk, wasted.
Smelling like cigarettes and perfume,
Red lipstick smeared all over your perfect pink lips.
But I didn't care because you were back,
I'd clean you, feed you, dress you,
And you'd tell me how much you love me.

But it was all a lie.
Everything you said to me,
Means nothing now.
Because you can never come back,
From what you did to me.

You hurt me,
And I don't know what to do.
You'd say you're sorry
But I knew better than that.

I fell into your trap.
An endless cycle of of *I'm sorry's* and *I love you's*
Mean absolutely nothing anymore.

I loved you
You loved me,

But we had a love that wouldn't last.

# THE ROSE OF ME

## By Jayson Mitchell

Doing nothing more than sitting and thinking.
I gaze up at the starry sky with tears in my eyes,
What have I done to be forsaken so.

All of these things I can't let go-
They haunt me everywhere I go...

I clutch this rose,
A beautiful rose.
It was once clean but now it's red,
The water runs onto this book too many times read.
I say that it's all in my head-
But if that be so then why do I look so dead.

I sit and I think,
A name echoes in this solemn place.
A name so sweet,
Like the smell of the rose-
A name to make its source.
Be it that this person ever returns,
And should my feelings still churn,
Present this rose with all its beauty.

I may be a beast but love I still carry-
I sing alone every night,
The song we sang that starry night.
I sit and think,
I cry, and I cry, and I cry...
For you I always yearn,
But I will never learn.
You picked me up,
Time and time again.

Each coming time,
You dropped me and walked away.
Still I gather the pieces-
For you to fix once more.

You are my world,
All that I have ever known.
Why do you forsake me so?
For you I do all I could,
Yet you play me
Like a boy made of wood.
I dance to your pulls and tugs,
I fly around like a stupid fool,
I never learn and never will,
I want you to see my iron will.

As I sit and I think-
I remember the good old times.
I cry and I cry,
I never did get to say goodbye.
Forgotten in time, where am I now?
An eternity to sit and think,
An eternity to cry.
I always look back and wonder why,
Even with you I never did fly,
Instead I was left high and dry.

No love was left-
Everyone had already left,
Cast away and broken inside.
Hell, why don't I finally die?

I write my last letter,
I read it over with tears in my eyes.
I clutch this rose for the final time-
I don't want to die,
No, no I don't.
But I hear that voice tell me so,
Nobody cares, nobody knows,

Just hurry up and let it all go.

My letter now drenched,
It's hardly legible-
I quickly scribble a new one.
The voice keeps asking me why,
Nobody cares, nobody knows,
That letter will just float off into the sky.
I crumple and throw it in exasperation,
Clutching the rose tighter,
My head getting lighter.
A red puddle at my feet,
Water pouring from my arm and hand,
I pass out but wake again oh too soon.

Nobody knew, nobody cared,
I went on lived my life.
A year goes by and I'm still alone,
An empty room,
Just me, this rope and a chair.
As I lay out the ugly affair,
I look up and stare,
Nobody will know, and nobody will care.
I climb onto the chair.
Stick my head through the rope,
And I drop off into the air.
I don't know why the rope had snapped,
But something within finally snapped.

That name as sweet as the rose,
Still lingered in my head.
It made it so I couldn't go to bed.
I sit and I stare,
I do nothing but stare.
As I stare-
I think,
As I think-
I cry.
Oh please come back,

Reality is losing slack.
I can't go on anymore,
These voices tell me I'm nothing more.

I scream and yell,
What the heck is this hell?
I remember that rose,
That once beautiful rose.
I see it there in a dark corner,
It sat for years-
Beside me through all my tears.
I smile a dreary smile,
Although I may be gone,
This rose shall always live on.
It is my life,
It is my friend.
Through all of the strife,
Until the very end.

# THE RED WOLVES

## By Jenny Nguyen

SAHAR WRAPPED HER WHITE shawl around her face as the desert winds picked up. Gold sand blew across the dunes and the setting sun cast long, dark shadows on the uneven bodies of sandstone. The girl led her travelling camel through the dry landscape at a weary pace. Bundles of scrolls, tattered books, enchanted gems, and potion vials hung in satchels on its furry sides.

They had trekked through the desert for days. Water was scarce, exhaustion weighed down her body, and her mind was plagued with loneliness. The last settlement she had reached had driven her out when she showed the locals her magic, calling her the "Devil's Child." Sahar frowned at the memory. They had been so welcoming of genies, fortune tellers, and witch doctors--but one look at a Marked Sorceress and they pick up their blades and torches. Sahar rubbed the dark tattoos that coiled around her tan arms: a pair of black cobras that began around her upper arms and curled down to end with their fangs outstretched at her wrists. She was a magician, a powerful sorceress, a warrior. It made people fear her—the "Devil's Child."

Her anger and pain gradually melted, leaving only sadness behind. Sahar didn't choose to be born this way. She didn't want to be dangerous. The young woman had run away from her coven because she couldn't stand the violence. The killing. The blood on her hands. She shivered and wiped her hands on her robes, as if trying to wash away the invisible death that stained her skin. Who could accept her, much less love her, when she carried such a dark past? She bowed her head and trudged on through the mountains of sand that crawled up her ankles and whipped against her hair, unsure whether the "home" she was seeking even existed.

\* \* \*

The night settled and stars shone like twinkling jewels against the vast, black sky. The chilly air echoed with the distant cries of coyotes. Sahar rubbed her eyes as she continued to stagger forward, half-asleep.

"Almost there," the girl murmured to herself, not exactly sure what "there" was. She would know once she reached it, whatever "it" was.

After another mile, something bright glimmered on the flat, dark horizon like a jewel nestled in a rock. A fire, perhaps? Or lanterns from a small house. Either way, light meant warmth, and warmth meant company and food. Hope blossomed in her chest and tugged on the reins of her sleepy camel before tottering off towards the burning light.

As Sahar came closer, she heard the whistle of a flute and the beat of multiple drums pounding away with the rhythm of her heart. The pleasant sound of people singing and laughing filled the cold air and chased away her misery. Sahar made a few steps towards the music, towards the wonderful promise of company, but halted before she could go into full stride.

What made her so sure these people would welcome her? Wasn't she exiled from the last kingdom she set foot in? The girl remembered the blades, the curses, and the fires all too well. Did she even deserve to be with other people after all she'd done? She took a fearful step back into the dark. She did not. The only place in the world that waited faithfully for her was hell.

As Sahar turned to leave, a bizarre dizziness struck her. She leaned on her camel to steady herself, yet the world continued to spin. Shouts pierced her ears, their words unintelligible. The music had stopped and dark figures were approaching her from the fire. A wild fear seized her heart.

"No," she warned them, her voice hoarse, "don't come near me." She tried to shout at them, to run away, but her head felt heavy and her feet stayed glued to the sand. Her eyelids fluttered and she fell to the sandy ground. The last thing Sahar saw before the darkness swallowed her was the burning fire, and a pair of gentle hands reaching towards her.

* * *

Sahar stood on the outskirts of a burning village. For how long, she did not know. Thick, black smoke blanketed the crimson sky. Terrified screams filled the air as villagers fled their crumbling homes.

"Please...help me." A young boy limped up to her. His tattered clothes were stained with blood and his eyes were wide with fear. "I can't find my mother."

Sahar tried to reach out for him and bring him into the safety of her arms, but her hands were stuck to her sides. She couldn't move--her limbs felt as if they were made of lead.

"Please, miss. I'm scared. I--" A black knife pierced his back and went through his chest. Sahar watched in horror as dark flames erupted from the wound, eating up the boy's body like an infection. He fell to the ground, face blank with death, a silent scream on his lips.

Sahar's body went cold when she saw the killer. A dark-haired girl wearing a sleeveless black shirt and pants reached down to pull the dagger free from the boy's rotting corpse. Her arms were blood-stained and dark with soot, but Sahar could still see a pair of curling snakes swimming through the girl's bronze skin.

173

*She was the murderer.*

"No," she gasped. Tears blurred her vision as she watched herself kick the boy's limp body before chasing down another fleeing villager. The screams of her victims filled the air and she was powerless to stop it.

"I'm sorry." She wept at the dead bodies of the villagers. Their empty eyes stared at her in silent accusation, drilling guilt and self-hatred into her soul. *'You did this to us,'* their slack, bloodied mouths cried. Tears streamed down Sahar's cheeks.

"Please, I didn't understand what I was doing," she pleaded, but it was hopeless. No one could forgive her. No one.

* * *

"I'm sorry." She croaked.

"For what?"

Sahar flinched as something nudged her shoulder.

"Hey, wake up."

Sahar opened her eyes to find a girl with black hair and warm, honey-brown eyes gazing down at her. Her pale skin glowed in the dim light and a jade necklace glimmered on her slim neck. A slight accent brushed her soothing voice when she spoke.

"You looked like you were having a nightmare," she said, gently padding Sahar's sweaty forehead with a damp towel. "You've been asleep for two days."

Sahar blinked in confusion. The fire, the dead villagers, and the thoughts of her dark past were all slipping away like water through cupped hands. She shifted her body to sit up on the bamboo bed. The scent of sweet incense laced together with something metallic filled the air. Behind the other girl sat a bronze statue of a man with a wolf's head sitting cross-legged. Three thin burning sticks sat in an ornamented gold jar in front of it, alongside a fresh offering of animal carcasses.

"My camel...my belongings..." she said as she rubbed her eyes.

"They're right over there," the girl said, pointing to her bundles of precious vials and runes stacked neatly by the flapping entrance of the tent. "And your camel is being taken care of by some *curious* young soldiers outside." She said with a soft laugh.

Sahar leaned back her head in relief. "Thank you. And who are you? Where am--?" She coughed dryly.

The girl grabbed a wooden cup by the bed and held it to Sahar's mouth. "Call me Chunhua." Her rosebud lips perked into a small smile. "You're in the camp of the Red Wolf tribe."

*The Red Wolf tribe?* Cool water slid down Sahar's throat and she closed her eyes in bliss, letting the liquid refresh her. Yesterday night's events returned to her in a slow blur. The dreadful miles upon miles of struggling through sand, the light gleaming from afar, the dancing people and flute music, the reaching shadows.

"I've never heard of such a tribe," Sahar said. "But I owe your people a great debt." She looked down at herself. Her clothes had been replaced with a shirt made of linen that exposed her arms. She looked back up at Chunhua.

"Do you know what I am?"

"Of course." Chunhua replied.

Sahar's body tensed and she furrowed her brows. "And you don't want to kill me?"

"Why would I?" The girl asked, tilting her head. "It was one of your kind that had saved our tribe many years ago. This is the least we can do to thank your people."

Sahar's eyes widened. Marked Sorceresses don't save lives. They only killed, looted, and destroyed them. "What do you mean?" Sahar asked, her voice full of disbelief. "I think you've got the wrong idea."

"Nonsense." Chunhua said, rising from her chair before taking Sahar's hand and smiling. "You must meet my brother. He has been asking for you all day. Everybody has."

"I…" Sahar stopped in the middle of her protest, deciding it was wiser to wait to hear their story first. Besides, she missed having people to talk to. She let the other girl pull her out of bed towards the light streaming into the tent.

Sahar gasped when she stepped outside. Dozens of large, crimson tents stood over the soft desert sand. Men and women donning light bronze armor were dueling with scimitars, daggers, and swords under the beaming sun. Others were running laps around the camp while some relaxed in the shade.

Those who passed by eyed Sahar with a mixture of curiosity and awe, before whispering to their comrades in a strange language she couldn't understand.

"This is a military camp," Sahar realized. "Where is your tribe from?"

"Lotus. We traveled here from the northeast to discuss a peace treaty with the kingdom of Enzia," Chunhua replied.

The two girls approached a wooden pen where two men were dueling. One wore a crimson-horned mask of a demon's head, while the other wore a red blind-fold. Behind the ring stood drummers who beat against round drums adorned with bells. The steady rhythm added to the intensity that vibrated in the hot air. The two opponents kicked up sand as they circled each other in anticipation.

"This is a traditional game we always play: Catch the Demon," Chunhua said, her eyes bright with excitement.

The man in the demon mask leapt forward, swinging his sword down in a cutting motion. The blindfolded man lifted his sword up horizontally, and caught his attacker's blade with a loud "clang" just before it could reach his head. He kicked the "demon" back, forcing it to stagger.

"How can he fight back without seeing?" Sahar asked, amazed.

"He calls the wolf spirits for guidance," Chunhua said. "We worship the *Láng* god with offerings of fresh meat and blood. In return, he gifts us with his wolf spirits who aid us in battle. Those who can master the art of communicating with the spirits can use them to do what ordinary humans cannot."

With a yell, the blindfolded man charged forward. Sahar gasped when she saw wispy, fragmented images of silver wolves chasing after his blade. He swung his gleaming sword at the "demon," sending its sword twirling out of his hand in a flurry of sparks kicking his opponent to the ground.

"Caught you." He said with a grin, pointing his blade at the other man's chest. The "demon" raised his hands in surrender and the spectators cheered. They climbed over the wooden bars and ran up to the victor, praising him for his skill.

"I hate playing the *Yaoguai*; you know how hot this mask is?" The other man got to his feet with a groan and pulled off the horned mask. He was a stout, bearded man with twinkling eyes and a friendly face. A thin scar ran along the side of his eye.

"Oh come on, Peng. You almost had me." The victor laughed, pulling off his blindfold and putting a comforting arm around his friend. He had short, dark-hair and warm brown eyes.

"Brother," Chunhua called through cupped hands. "Brother Duck, waddle over here, will you?"

The man looked up at the two girls, still laughing, and his eyes went wide when he saw Sahar. After nodding gratefully to his cheering peers, he walked ever to them with Peng by his side.

"Chunhua, I wish you wouldn't call me that in front of guests," he said before bowing to Sahar. "I am General Zhang Jianyu of the Red Wolf tribe, son of Commander Zhang Feng. But please, call me Jianyu."

"And I am Captain Xi Peng. It is an honor meeting you," Peng said while also bowing to Sahar.

Sahar blushed from the attention and bit her lip. A well of guilt opened up in her chest.

"I'm Sahar. But I don't think you fully understand who I am. But I...I'm grateful for your hospitality, nevertheless," she stuttered. She cringed at her words once they left her mouth.

"Jianyu was the one who found you." Chunhua nudged her brother with an elbow. "You should have seen the way he took care of you all these nights after his duties. All gentle and tender-like--"

"Okay, little sister, I think it's time for your beauty sleep," Jianyu said hurriedly and tried to push Chunhua away.

"Oh, that was you?" Sahar said, her cheeks turning red. "Thank you for your kindness."

"It was not a problem." Jianyu scratched the back of his head and looked away. An awkward pause followed.

"I think I'm going to get something to eat." Peng patted Jianyu's shoulder.

"I'll join you, Peng," Chunhua said, looking back and forth at Sahar and her brother. "Have fun you two." Before either of them could protest, Peng and Chunhua hurried away down the busy line of tents and vanished into the crowd of people.

"So...Brother Duck, huh?" Sahar said, raising a brow at Jianyu.

"She's been calling me that since we were children." He laughed, tightening the sweaty hand wraps around his palms. "And...I've never fought a Marked Sorceress before." He continued, a sly grin forming over his lips.

"Consider yourself lucky." Sahar replied. It was half-jest and half-truth.

"Well, looks like today I've run out of luck." He said, and threw the sword Peng had dropped to Sahar. The girl caught it out of the air and twirled it in her hand. It was beautiful. The sunlight gleamed off its edge, illuminating the trail of carved wolves that ran towards the tip.

"I'm not so sure, I haven't held a sword in years," she said with reluctance. In truth, her heart was pounding with both the excitement and dread at the thought of combat. She could feel the snakes crawling under her skin in response to the weapon she held, ready to strike. It was all too familiar. Sahar shivered.

"Well, alright then. Didn't expect much from a girl who couldn't make it out of the desert by herself, anyway," he teased and sheathed his sword.

Sahar's mouth fell in shock. *Who does he think he is?*

She let out a rueful chuckle before leaping over the wooden bars to where Jianyu stood with his arms crossed.

"Unsheathe your sword, *little general.*" She raised her blade in a challenge. "Let me show you what happens when you tempt the cobra."

Jianyu grinned in triumph and backed up into position.

"I've killed many snakes before. Try me."

The two rushed at each other with their swords raised. A shower of metal sparks followed as they clashed. Sahar slashed at Jianyu, who parried before swinging back. The girl dodged and kicked; the young man blocked and swung again. They dove at each other, yelling insults and unpleasantries as they traded swings. One attacked while the other countered which would then be dodged and reflected again. A scratch here, a torn shirt here, and a bruise there.

A crowd of soldiers had gathered to watch their general duel the mysterious sorceress. Chunhua and Peng had returned. Bets were made, but were eventually abandoned when the spectators realized the match wasn't going to end anytime soon. Even with the help of magic and spirits, Sahar and Jianyu were equally matched. As the sun went down and the moon rose, the soldiers left to their tents and posts, leaving the two alone under the moonlight.

"Aren't you...tired yet?" Jianyu panted as he sent a half-hearted punch at Sahar's shoulder. She didn't even bother to dodge it.

"Not...in the...slightest," Sahar said while kicking Jianyu. He crumpled to the ground, groaning, and Sahar collapsed with him. They flopped onto the cool sand next to each other, laughing in between their moans of pain.

"I won that," Sahar said, savoring the soft sand and cool wind that kissed her bruised skin.

"I'd say it was a tie," Jianyu replied, turning his head towards her with a smile. The moon glinted off his dark eyes and sweaty skin.

For a while, they just laid there next to each other, basking in each other's presence and gazing up at the serene stars. A tranquil flute song danced along the breeze from Chunhua's tent. Sahar had never felt so peaceful in her life. It was as if the sweat had washed away her worries in a way tears never could. Or perhaps it was the warm eyes and teasing smile of the general beside her that soothed the sharp edges of her broken life.

"You should join us." Jianyu said thoughtfully. "We can use someone with your skill."

Sahar inhaled softly, and let silence fill the air as she thought.

"Not unless you want to, of course." Jianyu said hastily and rose up on his elbows to look at her. "It would be nice if you stayed. You can help train the cadets and fight off intruders. We'll get you initiated into the tribe. My father won't mind. We'll even teach you how to communicate with the spirits. It'd be good for Chunhua, too--she likes you." He paused. "I like you."

Sahar's eyes widened and her heart leapt at his words. This was what she always wanted--to belong somewhere, to have people to love, and a place to call home.

She was about to jump on Jianyu and pull him into a hug before a thought pierced her heart. Would Jianyu still accept her once he learned about her past? What will he do when he finds out about the innocent souls she's taken from this world? She got to her feet.

"I thank you for your kind words, Jianyu. But I can't. I don't deserve to be here. "

"I don't understand," he said, confused.

It pained her to hear the hurt that stained his voice. She sighed and held out her palm in front of him. "Years ago, when I fled from my coven, I pledged to myself I would never use my magic to kill another being again." The snake tattoo that painted her skin began glow and shift as she called it forth. The black ink slithered down her arm and pooled into her palm, from it, rose the dark head of a live cobra. "We killed people. Murdered them in their homes. This was what we were taught to do since a young age. My coven leader said we were doing the right thing, that the gods were praising us for weeding out the weak." The cobra in Sahar's hand disintegrated itself to form a dark dagger with a curved edge and fang scratches on the metal. The blade glowed with purple flames that threw grotesque shadows on the sand.

"It wasn't until many years later I realized how terrible we truly were. But it was too late. No one who knew about the Marked Sorceresses would take me in. And that's how it should be." She crushed the dagger in her fist, and it crumbled into dark ashes before slithering back up her arm as an inked brand of her sinful bloodline.

Jianyu was silent. The darkness of the night made it impossible to read his face. Sahar didn't want to. She turned to leave.

"I'll go before sunrise." Her voice cracked. "Thank you. For everything."

Before she could make it over the wooden bars, Jianyu's voice called out to her.

"Wait."

Sahar halted and balled her fists, her heart pounding.

"You think you're the only one with regrets?" A flash of light came from behind her, followed by a low growl. She spun around to find a large silver wolf with azure markings painted on its face, sitting beside Jianyu, who was kneeling and stroking the beast's fur. The wolf stared at Sahar with icy blue eyes that seemed to look right through her.

"This is *Xun*, a wolf spirit. She chose to be my guardian the night before my first battle and has fought with me ever since." Jianyu scratched the wolf under her chin and she closed her eyes. "I used to have two guardians. My first one, *Jin*, he came to me after I saved my sister from drowning in a frozen lake that cracked. It's rare thing for a human to be chosen by a spirit, much less two. The entire tribe was so proud." He laughed from the memory, but it was a sad laugh.

"What happened?" Sahar asked. Jianyu was silent for a moment.

"He abandoned me when we attacked the Enzian camp. As it turned out, the enemy soldiers had stayed in a village, a village full of innocent civilians trying to survive through the war. I didn't feel the need to send out a scouting party first to survey the camp. It was a careless mistake. A *devastating* mistake. One that cost hundreds of innocent lives." His eyes darkened and his eyebrows knit together in shame.

"But even with blood on my hands, I didn't run away." He looked up at her. "As long as my body could still fight and my voice could still lead, then I shall keep on living, fighting. If not for my sake, then for them." He pointed his chin at the tents that lined the sand. "Not a day goes by where I don't hate myself for what I've done. But what can I do? Life pushes me forward and I still have people to protect." He rose to his feet.

A series of howls broke through the night. Long, echoing cries floated with the wind from afar. Warm lights speckled the dark dunes as soldiers left the bright comfort of their warm tents and ran into the chilly air, carrying weapons and donning bronze armor. Blood-red wolf masks were pulled over their faces.

"General Jianyu," Peng called from a tent, an axe in his hand. "The spirits tell us intruders are coming from the west. The commander orders we stay and fight." Jianyu nodded and picked up his sword. Xun let out a powerful howl before disappearing into the air in a flush of wind and silver light. The man climbed over the wooden bars and turned to face Sahar. His jesting smile had gone, replaced by a serious expression of a general. Yet, his brown eyes were still warm.

"Maybe you can't rewrite your past, but the story hasn't ended yet." He reached out his hand in front of her, like an offering. A choice. "So how will you end yours?"

Sahar looked towards the horizon, where the first rays of dawn peeked over the sandstone and chased away the dark sky with its rose-gold brilliance. The dark cobras that lived inside her ached to be released, to fight. And like the ancient sorceress that saved the tribe many years ago, she can fight for the right thing--to protect her friends.

Sahar took his hand.

# IF ONLY YOU KNEW

## By Mikayla Reilly

I find you in the corner,
Head cupped in your hands,
Covering your beautiful face.

You are crying.
Streaks of tears mark your face,
Dulling and killing your bright, blue eyes.

You're being comforted
But nothing stops the tears,
Your sorrow seems never ending.

I once cried your cries
And felt your sorrow,
So let me help you.

Don't shut me out,
Please, let me help you.
Hear what I have to say:
You are beautiful even with your flaws
You are loved and accepted by so many,
You are worth it, if only you knew.

# STILL SLEEPLESS

## By Becky Lee

It's 3:00 A.M., and I'm still awake.
I cannot sleep, I cannot move.
One little peep will wake them up.
These crazy thoughts run through my head.
They're loud, and they're obnoxious.
"Do this, do that. Maybe, get a snack."
I don't want a snack. I want to sleep,
But you're keeping me from that.
I try my best, but my mind digresses from
The thought of actually sleeping tonight.
Before I even know it, the orange and pink
Hues of the shining sun hit my windows.
This is just great. Another night wasted, and
I'm still sleepless.

# NIGHTINGALE

## By Kimberly Nguyen

There once was a tree behind my abode
With branches that stretched far beyond the road
Its leaves a deep green and its bark thick and sturdy
It was home to a small little birdy.

A little nightingale with a voice loud and bold
Whose charming songs live in stories of old
Her voice pure and forthright
Through the terrors of night
She kept me sane when nothing was right

There came a day, one much like today
When my nightingale simply flew away
With her tawny wings extended
Time became suspended
As I watched from my porch in the beautiful month of May

It's been years since that day
And forever I will stay
In this humble abode
Where I met a little bird so bold
As to sing all my worries away.

# GO ON

## By Vicente Inciong

I'll listen to you for as long as you need
My mind and heart invested in what you say
I could do this all day
But I don't even know why.

I feel like I could push beyond my own limits,
Break barriers and overcome obstacles,
My heart beats faster at the sound of your laughter
But I don't even know why.

Even the most tedious and tiresome of days
Are reversed and turned into symphonies, into light-hearted play
When I see you come my way
But I don't even know why.

I don't understand how someone can make me this happy
When I know that I can't return all that energy
But I know that someone else--that he--can

I hope he loves your stories as much as I do
I hope he enjoys your laugh as much as I do
I hope he sees just how lucky he is. I do.
Because you can give him all this happiness,
And he, he can give it back to you.

But I stand here still and let you go on
I still partake in whatever joy you can emanate
Knowing that your favor is not for me
But for someone else.

So go on, please
Keep doing what you always do

Be beautiful, and I'll keep humoring you
Without really knowing why.

# SISTERS

## By Gabrielle Romero

"YOU'LL NEVER GET ME to tell you where the jewels are," Ally said. She jabbed a finger at my shoulder. She flared her nostrils and furrowed her eyebrows, and the corners of her mouth twitched. I would call her out on it, but I didn't have time to be her acting coach.

"Save it for drama club. Just tell me where you put my ring. I know you borrowed it last night." I looked her in the eyes, letting her know I meant business. Mom taught me this. She knew that Ally would be a handful in high school, and mom was rarely ever wrong. Even when she's gone, she's still right.

Ally sighed. "You used to be fun, Alex," she said, reaching into her purse. "And it's Mom's ring. You can't just claim it like a dog pissing on its territory." She grabbed my wrist and slapped mom's diamond-studded wedding band in my palm.

I ignored her comment and continued to pack my clothes for tomorrow. I was spending the night at Kristine's house to celebrate her 18th birthday. I slept over every year. We would bake and watch movies all night long. This was the first year Mom wouldn't be driving me there. It felt wrong to not have a piece of her with me.

"You're going to be home right?" I asked. "Dad needs help moving Mom's stuff."

Her hands were on her hips. She looked down at the floor and then up at the ceiling, running her tongue across her bottom lip. "Yeah, I'll be here." She nodded her head while looking anywhere but at me. "Tell Kristine I said happy birthday." Without even a proper goodbye, she made a beeline to her bedroom.

\* \* \*

I sat down in my car, plugged the aux cord into my phone, and blasted my music on to alleviate the silence. The first song, *LA Devotee* by Panic! At the Disco, played. I let out a tired laugh. My eyes stung as I replayed the memories of my adventures driving down Hollywood Blvd. I pictured Mom in the driver's seat shaking her head at Ally and me while we sang our hearts out. Through the rolled-down windows, we blasted our music for everyone to hear whether they liked it or not. Ally held my hand, serenading me to the song that represented everything we felt when the three of us were together. It was the same feeling I got whenever we couldn't stop laughing at one of Ally's stupid jokes. She was always the center of attention, but it was well deserved. Everything Ally said caused an eruption of laughter. Her smile then was ten times bigger than what I've seen this past year. I missed that smile. I missed laughing. My chest felt like it was holding up the weight of the world. Well, at least our world.

I stopped and stared at the traffic light as it cast a red hue over the street. Everything else seemed less important than that bright, red light. You'd think it'd catch anyone's attention before they went on to speeding into oncoming traffic, but I guess other people's lives didn't matter when you were intoxicated. My knuckles turned white as I gripped the wheel harder. We all make mistakes, but most people's mistakes don't end lives. Forgiveness was a journey, but I wanted to forget about it just for tonight.

I pulled into Kristine's driveway and immediately wanted to put the car in reverse. She stood in a tight black dress while waving at me from her window. That was not sleepover attire. I got out of the car and threw my hands in the air. "What are you wearing?" I yelled.

She held up her finger, motioning me to wait. God, I could hear the sound of her heels hitting the wooden stairs as she rushed out of her house to my car. She reached through the window and hugged me.

"Hey, Alex!" She opened my car door, and for a second, I thought she was going to turn off my car and unbuckle the seatbelt for me. "C'mon! C'mon! I have something to show you." She dragged me out of my car, into her house, and upstairs to her bedroom. She sat me down onto her computer chair and shoved my head forward until it was only inches away from her laptop screen. The brightness made my eyes burn.

"Kris, I can't read it like this. I'm going cross-eyed." I laughed as she groaned at my unenthused tone of voice. I backed up and read the Facebook message from Danny, her lifelong crush and my childhood friend. It was an invitation to a party at his house. I looked up at Kristine, and her face said it all. We were going to this party whether I liked it or not.

"Danny Rodrigues invited us to a party. We have to go!" She jumped up and down like a child begging for candy.

"Oh, yes. My oversized sweater and basketball shorts agree." I shook my head at her.

"You can borrow an outfit. Just please, please, please can we go?" This woman was on her knees now, and her hands clasped together as if I was about to decide her fate. Maybe in her mind I was.

I rolled my eyes and pulled her up. "Fine, but no alcohol. And, if given the chance, you must not leave me for Danny. Understand?" She nodded her head vigorously. "Okay. Let's do this."

She found me a sequin top and the tightest pair of leather shorts she could find. I drove us to Danny's house, adjusting my shorts every few minutes. I have always admired Kristine for pulling off these outfits, but wearing them myself was a different story.

The moment we turned on to the street, we saw people running into their cars. Seemed like the party got broken up. *Oh, darn. What a shame.* I stopped my car in front of Danny's driveway, where he was yelling at people to leave.

"Hey, Danny. What happened here?" I hadn't talked to him in a while, but it never felt foreign when I did.

"Hi, Alex. My parents just called, and they're coming home early from their trip. Sorry you guys missed the party." He bent over and waved at Kris in the passenger seat. "Happy birthday by the way." I looked at her. She was internally losing her crap.

She giggled. A quiet "hi," was all she could utter. He flashed her his well-known flirtatious smile, and she pretty much died and went to heaven.

Then he looked at me. "Are you here to pick up Ally? I think she and Brendon left a while ago. He said something about the gas station and then going somewhere else for the night. I didn't really catch anything after that." I snapped my head toward him, my eyes widening. She lied to me. She was out with Brendon? I know Brendon is Danny's little brother and she knows him like I know Danny, but why did they go to this party together? And now they were out somewhere in the middle of the night.

"How long have they been hanging out again?" I asked, still shocked.

"Oh, she's been coming to the house pretty often. She and Bren seemed to have reconnected. Maybe we can grab lunch sometime and catch up. We miss having the Walker girls around," he said.

The shock and anger subsided for a moment. I did miss him. Things had been so hectic since mom died, and I haven't had the chance to check in with them.

"Ally told me she was staying at home tonight. I think I'm going to look for her and bring her home. Want to come?"

He pursed his lips and looked back at his house. "Busting your sister sounds fun, but I have to clean the house before my parents get home. We really should catch up though."

"Definitely. Good luck cleaning." I smiled and waved while driving away. I look over at Kristine. She was still in a trance.

"He knew it was my birthday," she said. She smiled as if it was all a dream.

"We all get a notification from Facebook. Everyone knows it's your birthday." And with that, I had crushed her dream.

I crept into the gas station with my headlights off, hoping they wouldn't be able to see me. I wanted to know what was going on between Ally and Brendon. Why did she lie to me?

I looked over, and the two of them were in Danny's car. They were about to drive away.

"What were they doing at the gas station?" I asked.

"Getting gas?" Kris was obviously giving them the benefit of the doubt.

"I bet they were getting condoms or something." The words stung my throat. Ally was only 15. She had better not been having sex already. I know I wasn't Mom, but I was going to give her the talk when we got home. She was going to parties and having midnight adventures without telling me. I knew this was going to be a problem. She could be so reckless sometimes.

I continued following them a few cars behind, my eyes laser focused. Kris and I had been creating a multitude of scenarios, and they kept getting worse and worse. I'd somehow already come up with a babysitting schedule for their future unplanned child. Mom would be pissed at me if I let anything happen. I should have called Dad to check if she was home. I followed them into a parking lot and realized we were at a dimly lit cemetery.

Do not tell me they're going to do it in the parking lot of a creepy graveyard. Come on, Allison. You're classier than that.

They got out of the car and started climbing over the fence. Ally held a plastic bag, and Brendon carried a blanket.

"Are you kidding me? They're going to do it *in* the cemetery? That's disgusting and morbid." Bile rose in my throat. Kris took my hand and pulled me toward the fence. I wrapped my fingers around the fencing and looked through, ready to stop them if things started to get weird. Brendon unfolded the blanket and smoothed it out on the ground in front of a headstone. The headstones were lined up in uniform, some taller and newer than others. There was a sad, leafless tree that looked like its droopy branches were reaching out for a hug behind them.

My eyes grew wide. It was a tree I'd leaned on for comfort many times this past year. I took a step back and looked at the sign on the fence. "St. Mary's Cemetery." I looked back at them and saw Ally laid flowers in front of our mother's headstone as Brendon wrapped his arms around her. I was stupid, really stupid. I glanced at Kristine and saw tears well up in her eyes. She knew I was stupid too. I wrapped my arms around myself as I watched Ally and Brendon just sit and hold each other. That should've been me. I should've been the one comforting my sister, not going on a goose hunt, thinking she was going to have gross car sex.

She needed me. Out of all the scenarios I conjured up, I couldn't believe I didn't see that coming.

# OD

## By Alex Quang

Travel through this tunnel
Your music blasting loud
The euphoria invades your body
Like raving with the crowd

You feel it overtake all nerves
Every cell
Is screaming for more
You take one more hit
Before your body hits the floor

Your friend cries for help
Your mom cries for you
That's very tragic
But the fact you are gone
Is very tragic too

# THE EFFECT OF MUSIC
## By Angel Nunez

Music is important in my life, let me explain:
There hasn't been a day in my adolescence when I haven't listened to music.
I try to switch it up from time to time.
Rock, Hip-Hop, Jazz, Lo-Fi.
It doesn't matter. If it's good music, I'll listen to it.

I get into debates over what's good music--and what's not.
I try to find modern classics and hidden gems,
I go to thrifts and pick out random vinyls,
I see something interesting and pick it up.
I always look for Led Zeppelin or Rush in milk crates at swap meets,
But no success just yet.
As for CDs, well, I get what I know, 'cause
What I know, I like.

Ever turn off the lights, put on a cd or dropped the needle on wax, and just lie
down?
Close your eyes and really listen to the music?

I have. I know I have.
It's a good experience,
An hour of my life not wasted.
The songs I wasn't fond of become favorites,
I sing along off-pitch and make a fool of myself,
And the songs that are favorites become memorable.
Sometimes, a song comes on that I haven't listened to in a long time,
It's great,
Almost as if I'm listening to it for the first time,

Except this time, I know what to expect,
I'm anxious.
Anxious, waiting for that one part I like.

Meanwhile, I realize I neglected that one song and never recognized it for what it
is.


When the last song plays and I walk out of my room,
Two things happen:
My eyes adjust to the light,
And the world just seems different.
It just does.
Yeah,
It seems slower,
Then faster.
Trippy, right?
Behold,
The effect of music.

# RAPTURE OF THE GUILTY MIND
## By Jennifer Chau

Perhaps her mind had only wanted
to love one being at a time,
And so she broke both their hearts
and watched them die.

It was her guilty pleasure,
and one that she could not own,
For the heart
Is a complex thing
And one that the mind does not know.

But it was this feeling that it gave her,
The trickles down her spine,
The sorrow and the rapture,
The ones she could not define.

His lavender cologne,
The brush of his hair,
The way he smiled,
How could she not stare?

But the other boy's
Soothing voice,
His knack for a charm,
His silk smooth hair,
Was one to compare.

But stop--
Mind said,
Berating the heart,
Choose one, only one,
Or forget that they're there.

But her heart still took her,
With every inch of her body,
To love two beings,
Not one at a time.

And so she broke both their hearts
And watched them die.

# TARGETED

## By Kimberly Nguyen

SUNLIGHT BEAMED THROUGH THE office windows, stretching from the floor to the ceiling in rectangular rays. The air was thick with vapor that warmed the room until an unbearable, humid cloud rested on everything. Leaning over the desk, Sinclair shoved a dark clump of hair back into place with the swipe of his hand and continued to shuffle through the papers scattered across the mahogany desktop. He slammed his fists onto the desk and slumped back into his seat. The familiar sound of ringing phones and chatter filled Sinclair's office as Ava opened the door. Her lips raised to a quick smile before her eyes darted downward when the door clicked shut behind her. Sinclair straightened up in his seat.

"Any luck?" Ava leaned against the door.

"Nothing." Sinclair slid his fingers through his dark, sweat plastered hair.

"Well, you'll get it eventually." She looked down at the carpet.

He stared at her in silence. Feeling his gaze, she shuffled her feet, her eyes still glued to the dark carpet.

"What's wrong?" Sinclair asked while she continued fidgeting in front of him. "I know that look. What's bothering you this time?"

"I just don't know about the new case. It seems--" She glanced up at him. The familiar blue eyes urged her to continue. "--It just seems too dangerous."

"So, that's it." His fingers interlocked as he placed them on the desk. "Don't worry about me. The recent outbreak of murders has put everyone on edge. This article is just the thing to put us at the top. Besides, the Author wouldn't dare target me." He shot Ava a smirk, one she knew all too well.

"You're going after a serial killer. Do you really think that there aren't going to be any consequences?" Her gaze returned to the carpet. "It's dangerous."

"I'll be fine. Don't worry about me." Sinclair stood up and slid papers from the desk into his brown shoulder bag. He looked up at her. "I'm going to follow up on a lead. Call me if you need anything, okay?" He gave her arm a reassuring squeeze before leaving the room.

Sinclair climbed the spiraling staircase that led to his apartment, his shoulder bag flopping against his side at every step. Fumbling through his bag for a few moments, his fingers finally brushed up against the cold, sharp ridges of his keys. After unlocking the door, he heard the faint ticks of the kitchen clock float into the hallway. With the flick of his finger, Sinclair turned on the light switch. As if on cue, the shoulder bag slipped off of his shoulder and landed by his feet. He tossed his keys onto the shelf and slipped off his boots, settled in his favorite armchair with a sigh, and glanced at the clock. The informant should have called by now. Slouched on the armchair, Sinclair tapped his foot to the rhythm of the clock. He fidgeted, shifting his weight from side to side.

He focused on the bookshelf in front of him, studying the soft lines of the self-improvement books neatly placed in rows. The dimly lit room faded out of focus as the ticks of the clock intensified. *Tick, tock, tick, tock.* Sinclair counted the seconds. *Tick, tock, tick, tock.* His chest tightened. *Tick, tock, tick, tock.* He stretched, trying to shake the feeling away. *Tick, tock, tick, tock.* He moved his hands through his hair and circled them back down to cover his face. The clock seemed to scream at him from the kitchen wall.

A loud ring drowned out the angry ticks of the clock. He leaned his head toward the sound. The sound rung again, the sounds of the clock faded back into innocent clicks. It was the phone. He reached over and picked it up.

"Hello?"

"Sinclair?" a man's raspy voice said.

"Yes, this is Sinclair. Who is this?"

"You wanted information on the Author," he said. "Meet me at the corner of Brookdale and Cunningham in an hour."

"Wait--"

"--Come alone." *Beep, beep, beep, click.* The line went dead.

Sinclair slammed the phone back onto the receiver and rolled his eyes. "Why can't any of these people be normal for once?"

Shoving the mess of papers on the kitchen counter aside, he pulled out a piece of paper to scribble down the meeting place and shoved it into his bag still sitting by the door. He slumped back into the armchair, hoping to take a short nap before leaving. He closed his eyes and for a moment felt peace. From the silence of the apartment, a small click sounded from the kitchen, then another, and another. *Tick, tock, tick, tock.* Sinclair's eyes shot open. His head whipped toward the kitchen, his eyes narrowing in on the red clock hanging on the wall above the counter. *Tick.* The clock seemed to mock him. *Tock.* It criticized him for taking a break from work.

The torment of the clock became unbearable. He shoved his arms against the chair, lifting himself onto his feet. Moving in quick, wide strides, he went to the door, his arm swooped downward to pick up his bag and his keys jingled in protest as he grabbed them from the shelf. He strode out into the hallway, slamming the door shut behind him.

* * *

Boots sloshed through the murky puddles that blanketed the street, and dogs barked in the distance accompanied by the rattling of chain link fences. Sinclair clenched the strap of his bag that hung over his shoulder. He looked left to right as he stepped up onto the cracked curb. He arched his head to see two faded green street signs, each printed with white bolded letters. The few people who wandered the streets darted in and out of the light of the streetlamps that periodically appeared down the sidewalk. A single streetlamp stood several feet away from the street corner, its bulb flickering every few seconds with a hum. Sinclair leaned against the brick wall that rounded the corner and glanced at his watch. It was midnight--the informant was late.

As the darkness enveloped his body and chills ran down his spine, Sinclair wrapped his jacket tighter around himself. The distant sound of footsteps caught his attention and he straightened his posture. Emerging through the darkness was a figure, tall and slim. The face was veiled in shadows as the person approached. Sinclair clenched the bag even tighter, and a cold sweat ran down his face. In the street lamp's dim light, he could make out a small brown package in the figure's hands. As the figure approached the corner, Sinclair began to make out several sharp features on the figure's face. Just as the figure passed, the package was tossed at Sinclair's feet.

Sinclair peered at the package, unsure of what to do. Minutes passed. He loosened his grip on his bag, the blood rushing back into his hands. He reached for the package. Shoving it under his coat, he hurried back to his apartment.

Entering his apartment, Sinclair shook off his coat and made sure that the small brown package was still tucked safely in its pocket. He pulled the package from his coat and laid it on the dining room table before heading to the opposite end of the room to turn on the light. Sitting down at the table, he began unraveling the package from the brown packaging. It had become soaked from the wet ground. Peeling the soggy paper off, he pulled out a dark leather book. He slid his fingers across the backing, feeling the natural grooves of the leather; it was expensive. He flipped open the front cover of the book. A single line was scribbled on the white pages:

*You're next.*

The words seemed to jump from the page. Sinclair immediately recognized the handwriting. It was the Author's calling card. Every victim of the Author had received a book like this one, exactly three days before their death. He flung the book across the table with a flick of the wrist. The book slid across the tabletop, coming to a stop just before reaching the edge.

"Some informant. All they give me is this damn book as some kind of ridiculous joke." Leaving the book on the table, Sinclair dropped himself back into the armchair and flipped on the TV, refusing to acknowledge that the book ever existed. In the flickering lights of the TV screen, his eyes drooped, his breathing slowed, his head leaned to the side. As sleep took over, Sinclair thought he saw a dark shadow of a figure move behind the window of the front door.

* * *

The sun rose above the surrounding buildings, pouring light into Sinclair's apartment. A single ray of light shone directly on his face, waking him up. Extending his arms, Sinclair groaned as he stretched the aching muscles in his back. He pulled himself onto his feet and walked to the kitchen to grab a glass of water. Settling back into the armchair, Sinclair placed his glass on the table and placed his laptop onto his thighs. He began to pull up articles of the Author on the laptop when the screen went dark.

"Ugh. What happened?" Sinclair tapped the screen with his finger and the screen flashed on. For a moment the screen remained white, and then an image faded into view. The image of a young girl appeared. She was lying on her side, her auburn hair soaked in the pool of blood underneath. The screen grew dark again. He sat there frozen. Silence hung over the room as Sinclair attempted to process what he just saw. *It was a prank, it must have been. Maybe some kind of glitch.* The sound of the doorbell disrupted his thoughts. Sliding the laptop onto the coffee table, he left to open the door.

Standing at the door was a short, round man dressed in a khaki uniform lined with black. His hair was slicked back in an awful comb over in attempt to cover the bald patch on the top of his head.

"Good morning sir. I'm detective Johnson from the LAPD." The man flashed a gold police badge. "I'm sorry to inform you that your next door neighbor, Ms. Noh, was found dead in her apartment this morning. We were wondering if you have heard or seen anything unusual yesterday night."

"Oh my god..." Sinclair cupped his mouth. "H-how could this happen? She was such a sweet girl."

"I am sorry for your loss, sir. Were you close to Ms. Noh?" Detective Johnson asked.

"Not particularly. I usually only see her when heading out for work. She was a sweet girl, every once in a while she would cook dinner for me because, well, you see I live alone and sometimes I'm so busy with a new article that I forget to eat," Sinclair said.

"Oh, so you're a writer?" The detective scribbled something down in a notepad.

"A journalist for *Mysteries Monthly*," Sinclair answered, craning his neck to see what the detective was writing.

"So about my previous question--" Detective Johnson tucked the notepad away.

"--Oh... I was at home for most of the day, yesterday," Sinclair responded.

"Did you hear or see anything out of the ordinary?" the detective asked.

"Oh right. No, everything has been as it always has been, at least for all I know. I left the house at ten and didn't get home until almost one in the morning." Sinclair licked his lips.

"Mhmm." The detective was scribbling on his notepad again.

"If you don't mind me asking, but did someone do this to her?"

The detective peered up at Sinclair. "We're not sure yet but it is a possibility that she was murdered. We just want to cover all of the possibilities before we make conclusions. "

"If there's anything I can do to help, please feel free to contact me." Sinclair pulled a business card from the counter by the door and handed it to Detective Johnson.

"Thank you, and if you remember anything please call us." Detective Johnson turned to leave. "Oh, and we recommend that you stay in town for the next few days. Just as a precaution. We might need your statement again."

The detective walked down the hall to the next apartment, where Sinclair could hear him talking to the couple that lived next door. He shut the door and made his way back to his armchair. Remembering the laptop, he picked it up and placed it back onto his lap.

"What a shame. She was such a kind young woman," Sinclair said to himself. Just as he said this, the laptop's screen flashed on again, and this time it displayed a video. The same girl was there, but now she was facing the camera. His heart dropped as he recognized her as Heather Noh. She was pleading for her life. Tears streamed down her face as she stumbled backwards. The pupils of her eyes were narrow, revealing the bloodshot whites of her eyes. Erupting over her sobs was a gunshot. He watched as a whimper escaped Heather's pink lips, her torso swinging forward where the bullet entered her abdomen. Horrified, Sinclair saw her body flop onto the browned patterned rug, shriveling into the fetal position as a pool of blood gathered beneath her.

The camera zoomed in on her face, stricken white with fear. Sinclair could feel the muscles in his body shake, tears streamed down his cheeks and landed on the laptop screen which went dark again. Small white letters appeared on the screen.

### *Her death is on you Sinclair*

Sinclair jolted upward, dropping the laptop onto the ground. Veins bulged from his temples as he wiped the tears from his eyes.

"A joke, that's what this is. Someone's idea of a sick joke." He stood up but stumbled over his own feet and landed back in the armchair. Thoughts swirled in his head. *Did he just watch Heather die? Was it real? Should he go tell the police? No, they would think it was him. No, it wasn't him but he caused it. The Author. Yes, the Author. It was the Author.*

Sinclair rushed out the door, not even bothering to lock it. While walking down the street, Sinclair broke down what had happened one event at a time. As he walked, he felt as if someone was following him. He quickened his pace, now he was sure of it. Footsteps followed at his heels. Sinclair flipped to look behind him. There was no one. Continuing down the street, Sinclair found himself outside the library doors. Large stone lions stood at each side as if guarding the library. He entered the library, his eyes blurry as they adjusted to the dim lighting. Compared to the bustle of the street, he found the library's silence soothing. He pulled up a seat for himself at a table and for the first time realized that he had his bag with him. Images of the small leather book flashed in his mind, causing the fear to return to him.

"If he is going to target me, then I'm going to get to him first," Sinclair thought to himself. He pulled out images of the books sent to the Author's previous victims, analyzing the handwriting. The scribbles took on a life of their own and the horrid details of the murders became alive. He was convinced that the Author was behind it all.

Enveloped in thought with a new sense of motivation, Sinclair failed to notice someone sit down next to him. The figure cleared their throat.

"It's you." Sinclair looked up from the images.

"I've come to warn you," the figure responded. "You're next."

"Who are you?" Sinclair asked.

"He's after you, watch your back."

"Wha-what do you mean? How do you know this?" Sinclair asked. "Who are you?"

"You've seen what he has done to Heather. Don't let it happen to you." The figure stood up from the seat and walked down an aisle of books. Sinclair jumped from his seat and followed the figure, but by the time he turned the corner the figure had disappeared. He sighed and walked back to his seat. As he sat down, he noticed a small white paper was on the desk. He grabbed the paper and opened it. Scribbled on the paper in the same writing as the book was an address with the words:

*Better keep a close eye on her, Sinclair. You might just lose another one.*

Sinclair's eyes read over the address several times. It was familiar, but he could not place it. As he read over the address a third time, he realized that it was Ava's house. His hands fumbled through his bag searching for his phone. After finding it in the mess, he dialed Ava's number. *Beep beep beep.* The line was disconnected. Sinclair called again and still there was no answer.

"That damn girl never answers her phone." He slammed the phone down, grabbing his head in his hands before smacking the tabletop. He scooped the papers he had laid out on the table into his bag and rushed to Ava's house.

Arriving outside Ava's home, he immediately saw that something was wrong. Ava's garden was covered in yellowing grass, her prized flower bed shriveled and brown. Sinclair sprinted up to the doorway and repeatedly rang the doorbell. Drowsy, disoriented, and blinded by the sun, Ava opened the door.

"Sinclair? Wha--" Ava said.

"--Where have you been? I've been trying to call you all day. I--" he shouted.

Ava's brow furrowed. "What do you mean you've been trying to call me all day? You called me just 5 minutes ago and were spouting out nonsense."

"--I was so worried about you. Are you delusional? No one's heard from you all day." Sinclair said.

Ava pulled out her phone and showed him the call log, the small screen clearly showed a two minute long conversation with Sinclair just a few minutes ago.

"I don't remember talking to you."

"Sinclair," Ava placed her hand on his shoulder. "Are you alright?"

"I....I...I don't know," Sinclair stuttered.

"Come in. Let's get you a nice cup of coffee huh?" Ava smiled at him.

"No, no. I'm fine. Just need to figure some things out." Sinclair stumbled off the porch and went back to his apartment. He slammed his keys on the shelf by the table as he entered.

"What the hell is going on?" he screamed into the empty apartment. "The Author...he's behind all of this. He's messing with my head, that's all. He was the one who killed Heather. He was the one who threatened Ava and called her pretending to be me. It was him. All of it was him."

A loud bang from the other side of the apartment snapped Sinclair back to his senses. *It's the Author, he's here for me.* He turned and locked the door behind him and lunged across the living room to shut the windows.

"I'll get him before he can even touch me." Sinclair whispered to himself. The sound of footsteps echoed down the hallway to his bedroom. Reaching for his prized baseball bat, he positioned himself to charge whoever came through the hallway. He stood, his shoulders squared, back straight, elbows up. Sinclair gripped the baseball bat tighter as the footsteps grew closer.

*Thump, thump, thump.*

Sinclair could hear the heavy boots make their way toward him. Pressure built up in his chest as he held his breath.

*Thump, thump, thump.*

The heavy boots approached the living room. They were so close that Sinclair could almost see who it was.

*Thump, thump, thump.*

Sinclair's knuckles were white, veins bulged from his hands, and his body was rigid and leaning forward ready to charge.

*Thump*–then silence.

Silence hung in the air, Sinclair waited, holding his breath. Minutes passed. He decided to move to the hallway. Weaving around the cluttered room, he tightened his grip on the bat, turning his hands white. He was now at the edge of the hallway. In one quick movement he swung around the corner, screaming and swinging the bat back and forth. There was nothing there.

"Someone was here," Sinclair whispered to himself. "No, *he* was here. Author, you better show yourself! You'll be sorry you messed with me!" he screamed into the empty hallway. There's no response. Silence filled the apartment once again as he stood in the center of the hallway.

A chuckle rose from behind him.

"You thought you could escape me." Sinclair turned around to see the dark hooded figure.

"Get away from me," he said, waving the bat toward the figure.

"Silly little Sinclair. That bat won't save you. Your fate has been decided," said the figure.

"Who--who are you?" Sinclair asked. The hooded figure chuckled. He took a step toward Sinclair.

"Get away, I'm not afraid to hurt you," he whispered. From the dim light of the lamp, Sinclair could see the figure was smiling.

"Don't you see? You can't hurt me." The hooded figure inched closer. His face now visible in the light. The bat struck the floor as it slipped out of Sinclair's hands. The two stood in silence.

"Don't you see? I'm you." The figure leaned in and whispered into Sinclair's ear.

He was staring face to face with a mirror image of himself.

"No, this-this isn't possible." Sinclair staggered backward.

"It was you who killed all of those innocent people. It was you who murdered sweet little Heather." The figure pulled him closer. "And now, you must pay for what you have done."

"No wait--It wasn't me, it was the Author." Sinclair stumbled on his words. "It- it was you."

"I am you." the figure crept closer and closer to Sinclair who had fumbled his way into the kitchen. "You must pay for what you did." The figure reached for a knife that was placed on the kitchen counter. He lunged toward Sinclair.

* * *

The sound of sirens echoed through the empty streets. A young woman dressed in her nightgown with a blanket wrapped around her shoulders stood outside an apartment door talking to Detective Johnson.

"I-I don't know, I noticed a smell coming from the apartment and when I went to check if everything was okay--well you see the door was unlocked, and, and that's when--" The young woman broke down in tears. "I'm so sorry."

"It's okay. You've told me enough. Anyone would be shaken up after finding what you have. Please come this way miss." Detective Johnson led her away before climbing the staircase to an apartment door.

The door to the apartment was cracked open and a pungent smell filled the hallway. Detective Johnson entered the apartment and stood over the heap lying on the kitchen floor.

"You poor soul," he murmured.

Lying at his feet was Sinclair's body soaked in a pool of blood. On the living room walls letters were scribbled into the beige paint in ebony ink spelling out:

**The Author is within all of us.**

# SPIRIT OF THE RHINO

## By Vicente Inciong

I was out of options.
Faced with the new and the uncertain,
Couldn't backpedal any further,
The only way left was forward.

Everything that could've gone wrong went wrong.
Cornered with barely any room to think,
My flanks were blocked,
The only way left was forward.

I focused on what made me who I am,
On the things that made me laugh without a doubt,
On the things that made me cry without a sound,
The only way left was forward.

I set my hands down, planted my feet on the ground,
Lowered my head, repeated the names of the ones I loved,
Steeled every part of my soul to fear no darkness,
And charged forward.

# HURT
## By Kristy Diep

Dark thoughts run through your head
As you lay in bed
Wondering why they keep pushing you
Over the edge
You're on the brink
You pledge
To hurt no one
So you hurt yourself instead

Saved just in time
Your eyes are red
Lost and confused
Dazed
You take in the idea
That you were almost dead

Selfish attempt
Vicious in the moment spurs
You think it's for the best
But who are you to decide
Think about
A world without your presence

Take a step back
Gather yourself
Take a breath
Ponder for a moment
Take your time
You'll be okay

For I will be here
I will help guide you
I will forever hold you
If I must
Keep you safe
Be there through it all

I'll wait for a while
Till the day I finally see you smile

If you would just open the door
Allow me the opportunity
To help ease you
Let down your guards
Let me in
Through your head
To your darkest thoughts

# OPERATION FORLORN HOPE

## By Derek Nguyen

"KEEP MOVING, NO SENSE in giving up on the final stretch." The sergeant pulled out a pair of binoculars and peered at the columns of grey smoke rising from the horizon. "Fire teams Zulu and Delta gave it all they got, so we can keep going. Let's not disappoint them."

A private turned around and said, "With all due respect, sir, do you think just one squad can pull this off?" He pointed across the fields of brown wheat to the smoke. "We started off with three squads. Now it's just us, and we're down a man."

The sergeant climbed up the hill and stood next to the private. Putting a hand on his shoulder, he looked at the soldiers, who stared at him. "I don't know. But as long as I live, I'll see to it that the mission is carried out. And that all of you go home." He looked at the private, noting his glazed eyes. "I can't do that if our hope dies. Do you read me, Oliver Dubbo?"

The private licked his lips. "I read you loud and clear, sir." He shouldered his backpack and continued marching.

The sergeant took one last look at the columns of smoke. "For their sakes, for my own sake, let them go home in one piece." He sighed and turned to catch up with his squad.

Hiking through forests and slinking around the edges of clearings, the group made its way towards the remnants of a village. The sun had fallen below the horizon, and the sky transformed from light yellows and oranges to dark lavender. One of the soldiers knelt down, picking up a piece of scrap metal.

"Sergeant Murdock, take a look at this."

The sergeant strode over, taking the piece from her hands. "Is this paratrooper armor?" He flipped it around, noticing the dark green dragon etched on the titanium.

"Looks like it, Sarge." The soldier eyed the rubble strewn about the dirt roads. "The destruction seems recent, but there are no bodies." She aimed her rifle at the growing shadows. "Do you think we're too--?"

"Let's not jump to conclusions, Corporal Sanchez. Take half of the squad and search the houses. I'll take the other half to the church." He pulled down a visor over his helmet, bathing the world in green and white. "Maybe there are survivors that can tell us something."

She nodded and turned to the squad. Waving up three soldiers, her team veered to the left, using the forest for cover.

Murdock turned to the remaining men and women. "Weapons free, I don't know what's waiting for us." He waved the group forward, eying the bell tower of the church. Stars appeared in the sky, and darkness blanketed the village. The soft pattering of leather boots on dirt were sonic booms as the team made their way through the village.

In the maze of wooden beams and brick walls, there was evidence of a skirmish: shell casings in the streets, a broken knife stuck in a wall, and a helmet in a cottage. Its visor had a gaping hole, and on the wall behind it was a splattering of crimson paint. Murdock narrowed his eyes, following the bullet's trajectory up to the bell tower.

"Potential sniper up there." He turned to his team. "Dubbo, follow me into the church. You two stay here and keep watch on this street." The two soldiers broke formation, dashing through the demolished buildings.

Dubbo aimed at the tower. "I have you covered, sir. Let's move out." The pair sprinted across the street, wincing at each crunch of their boots. Leaning against the church doorway, they hesitated. Hearing nothing, Dubbo frowned and shook his head. "I don't like this. It's too quiet."

Murdock shrugged. "Only one way to find out if there's anyone inside." He kicked the doors open, swiveling his gun at the overturned pews and demolished altar. When nothing popped out, he peered up at the roof. Dubbo nodded and took point, crouch running to the door that led to the stairway.

Peeking underneath it, he shook his head. Opening the door, he aimed upwards, inching up the wooden steps. Murdock followed, noting the multiple windows spiraling up with the stairs. "They could've killed half of us before we even got to the town square."

Dubbo smiled. "Maybe there really is no one here." His smile faded as something rustled from overhead.

Murdock put a hand on his shoulder and took point, motioning for him to stay back. Peering under the bell tower's door, he saw a pair of brown military boots. "Flash!"

The boots swiveled towards the doorway. He could hear a faint clicking as the figure readied his rifle. "Thunder!" Murdock held up a hand to keep Dubbo back, then stood up and opened the door.

Looking back at Dubbo, he smiled. "Looks like I get to live for another day. Come meet a new friend." The private jogged up the stairs to see a paratrooper wave in greeting.

Murdock pointed at the man. "This is Corporal McCormick of the 78th Mars Airborne Division." Jabbing a thumb to Dubbo, he said, "We're part of the 34th Mars Ranger Regiment."

McCormick rubbed his stubble and nodded. "You're the force that's escorting ours to the extraction point, correct?" Seeing Murdock nod he stood up and gestured to the single road leading away from the village. "The others have holed up in a town about ten klicks down this road. I stayed in case your team happened to stumble upon this place."

He looked out at the town. "I saw two groups of four enter. Did you leave the other squads behind as a rear guard?" Noticing the rangers averting their gaze, he nodded. "I'm sorry. I shouldn't have--"

Murdock held up a hand. "It's alright, you didn't know. They knew the risks, and they were willing to take it." He adjusted the straps on his backpack and walked down the steps. "Let's go, before anyone knows we were here."

The trio stepped out of the church. The two sentries stepped out from the shadows, lowering their rifles when they saw McCormick. Murdock keyed his mike and said, "This is the Sergeant. We've got the package, rendezvous at the dirt road leading outwards, over and out."

When they got to the road, Sanchez and the others emerged from the undergrowth. Seeing the paratrooper, she nodded and motioned for her group to fall in, and the squad marched alongside the road. When the moon reached its zenith in the onyx sky, Murdock turned to the others, pointing to the trees.

In silence they set up camp, spreading out sleeping bags amongst the bushes. Murdock took first watch, lying prone in a bush. After two hours of listening to the wistful hoots of owls, he turned around to wake up Dubbo for his shift. Seeing him awake and sitting against a tree, he frowned and stood up. "Were you awake this entire time private?"

Dubbo jumped at his gruff whisper, shrugging in response. "Sorry sir, couldn't sleep." Seeing Murdock's stare, he sighed. "I was just thinking about the mission."

"What about it?" Murdock sat down next to Dubbo. "As your commanding officer I need to know what's bothering you." The private looked down the road.

"I was just thinking about what happens if we pull this off? What happens then?"

Murdock scratched his chin, following Dubbo's gaze. "*When* we pull it off, soldier. To be frank with you, I don't know. The war with the insurrectionists could end, or it can continue dragging on. But I'm leaning towards the former."

"What did the paratroopers find? Was it important enough for Zulu and Delta to give themselves up to buy us time?"

Murdock unslung his backpack and crawled into his sleeping bag. "You'll find out in the morning. For now, try not to fall asleep during your shift." He turned around in the bag, leaving Dubbo alone. The private opened his mouth, thought better of it, and laid in the bush. He didn't know that Murdock was still awake, making a silent prayer.

An hour before dawn, Sanchez woke the group up by blasting the saxophone solo from "Baker Street" at full volume through her media player. Seeing the group's sleep-muddled glares, she smiled and shrugged. "Sorry, but you know how the sarge hates dilly-dallying."

Murdock shook the ringing out of his ears and stood up. "Next time, I'll be the one blaring music down your ear. And it'll be heavy metal." Without further conversation the group broke camp, continuing their trek under semi-darkness and the veil of morning fog.

As pinks and oranges began to appear overhead, the soldiers arrived at the town. The fog rolled through the blown out buildings and rusted husks of cars. Apart from a raven perched on a broken streetlight, there was no other sign of life. McCormick stepped through the squad and motioned for them to follow him.

Navigating through the rubble, they stopped in front of a main street. Two apartment complexes lined the sides, creating a miniature canyon. McCormick eyed the windows, and then cupped his mouth. "Why do we need guns?!" His bellow echoed across the town, scaring away the raven. As the silence grew, he turned to Murdock. "They should be--"

"To save ourselves from harm!" A door opened on the left, revealing a paratrooper with a bloodied bandage wrapped around his head. "Corporal McCormick, I was beginning to think you weren't coming back." Seeing the others behind him, the soldier smiled. "I see you brought the cavalry. I'll lead you to the C.O." Walking up to the top floor, he knocked on the pine door. "Lance Corporal Vo, he's back." It opened, and a grizzled man stepped out.

"Thank you private." He nodded at Murdock. "I know why you're here. Come on in, I've got some news to share." The rangers looked at each other, and then followed the officer inside.

Men were milling around in the hallway, and in several rooms there were wounded sleeping on mattresses. McCormick looked at their gaunt faces and put a hand on Vo. "What happened here?" The lance corporal turned and looked at him. "That's what you're going to find out, sir." He opened the door to a living room, where radios and maps were stacked on tables.

"Welcome to our HQ. It's not the best, but it gets the job done." He sat down, motioning for the others to do so. When they all did, Vo faced McCormick. "Our position is compromised, sir. Last night, a group of insurrectionist commandos snuck past our sentries. We killed most of them, but one made it out." He reached into his pocket and pulled out an eyepiece. "I managed to access the files inside. Their objective was to eliminate us, and if they failed, two platoons would finish the job." Vo looked at Murdock. "I hope you have good news."

He fidgeted, avoiding the paratrooper's gaze. "Command sent three squads to escort you to the extraction point. Two of them didn't make it."

Vo cursed, slamming his fist on the table. "That's it then, huh? We can't hope to hold back two platoons with two and a half squads. Might as well surrender."

McCormick snorted. "You know we can't do that. The package is too important to lose to the enemy." He sighed, looking at the hallway of wounded men. "I'll die before I give it up."

Sanchez cleared her throat. "Pardon me for asking, but what is this package? I've been in the dark about this, and the sarge hasn't been too keen on spilling the beans."

Vo glanced at McCormick, who nodded for him to speak. "Command didn't want too many people to know about this." He leaned down and pulled up an armored briefcase, placing it on the table. "Inside this is the key to ending the war." Typing in a series of numbers on the touchpad, he flicked the latches and opened it.

Dubbo leaned in, squinting his eyes at the contents. "Is that…a list of all insurrectionist hideouts and strongholds? Complete with defense schematics and troop deployment?"

McCormick nodded. "Taken from them just two days ago. Command wanted the operation to be in complete secrecy, hence only a few selected soldiers knew anything about this. Like the C.O.'s from your squads."

Murdock grunted in assent. "That's why Zulu and Delta stayed back. It was an attempt to buy us time to reach the paratroopers to reinforce them."

"But we were mired down in bad luck the moment we landed behind enemy lines. What we have here is a fifth of what we started with." Vo leaned back in his chair. "A pair of VTOLs (Vertical Take-Off and Landing aircraft) are supposed to land two klicks behind the town at noon, but the platoons will be here by eleven. We'll be overrun by eleven-twenty with our current defenses."

"I'm sure we can hold them back for an hour." Sanchez looked at Murdock. "We can do that, right, Sarge?"

Murdock looked at a map of the town and crinkled his brow. "I have a plan involving the town's bridge and the center square. But this will need some coordination between us and the paratroopers…"

* * *

McCormick looked down from the bell tower to where Murdock and the squads were piling rubble on the streets. He keyed his mike and said, "Are you sure this will work?"

Murdock looked up at his position. "This is the only way we can slow them down. The wounded can't fight, so we need other ways to buy time. You and Sanchez just need to pick off their officers from up there. We'll do the rest."

Hearing the rumbling of a jeep, he turned around to see Vo and Dubbo hop off and walk over. "Are all the wounded at the evac?"

Vo nodded. "Left a couple of medics to watch over them." He turned and got back into the jeep, driving it across the bridge.

Dubbo walked absentmindedly up to Murdock, a pair of earphones plugged in his ears.

Murdock stared at Dubbo and said, "Private, what are you doing?"

Dubbo looked up and yanked them off. "Sorry Sarge, just listening to some music. I figured that if I'm going out today, might as well indulge myself."

"Don't say that." Murdock looked at the LCD readout on Dubbo's media player. "You listen to Gorillaz? I didn't think anyone apart from me listens to their songs anymore."

The private smiled, marching over to the rubble barriers. "Even though they were from sixty years ago, you've got to agree their songs are something else." He began packing the walls with bricks, filling in the gaps.

Murdock opened his mouth then his eyepiece flashed the message: **Enemy is entering town. ETA to your position is one minute.** He cleared his throat and said, "All right boys and girls, it's time to earn your pay. You know what to do." The soldiers nodded and sprinted to their positions, with Murdock and seven others crouching behind the walls. For a moment there was complete silence. Then they heard the unmistakable roar of engines.

The rumbling and clacking of treads on stone grew louder, and through a crack he saw two troop transports trundle into the street. He waited until three squads of infantry marched up beside them before he keyed his mike.

In the apartments above, six hands appeared over the windows, dropping grenades and Molotov cocktails on the hapless soldiers. As the flames and shrapnel consumed them, Murdock and the others rose from cover. Insurrectionists grunted and collapsed as bullets tore through their bodies, crumpling in heaps next to the burning vehicles.

Another wave of infantry poured into the street, and the firefight began. Bullets whizzed through the air and ricocheted off metal plating as each side took potshots at each other. Above the cracks of assault rifles and booms of shotguns rose the thunderclaps of sniper rifles.

Despite the crossfire, the insurrectionists continued to charge the defenders, forcing them to engage in melee combat. Murdock ducked as a bayonet flew overhead, grazing his helmet. His rifle kicked back, and the insurrectionist fell with a trailing moan. Looking up to resume firing, he saw another insurrectionist raise a bayonet to stab him.

The paratrooper that had greeted Murdock earlier shoved the sergeant aside. The bayonet flashed downward and slid into the paratrooper's neck. Before his body hit the ground, his comrades riddled the insurrectionist with lead. Rubble flew through the air as the enemy flung grenades into the apartments, and a ranger flew out of a window in a cloud of red mist. Murdock keyed his mike. "Everyone in the apartments, move to phase two."

Doors burst open as the soldiers dashed to the second defensive point, taking up positions in machine gun posts across the street in the town square. Murdock and his group lobbed a second volley of grenades over the walls to cover them, then retreated into the town square's buildings to continue the defense. "Top priority is keeping those guns alive; they're the ticket to our survival."

A boom echoed across the town, and a building exploded in a rain of wooden beams and bricks. Peering over a shattered window, he spotted a heavy tank crush the crude barricades under its treads, letting the insurrectionists pour into the square. It fired again, and a machine gun crew vanished in a fiery explosion. "Someone take out that damn tank now!"

In the building next to him a ranger rose to aim an anti-tank launcher, but was cut down with a hail of bullets. Murdock pointed to two paratroopers, who nodded and fired at the enemy while he dashed over to the launcher. Hearing bullets crack the paved stones under his feet, he dove through the broken door. Looking behind him, he saw the two soldiers slumped against a crimson wall. "Vo, activate phase three."

The tank moved into the square, firing another shell at the buildings. As the infantry surrounding it began to advance, Vo sprung his trap. Rappelling from the roofs, he and five others threw satchel charges on its vulnerable backside, and it went up in a red-orange blossom. Caught between the machine guns and Vo's ambush, the enemy infantry was cut down in droves.

Before Vo's team could catch their breath, another tank smashed through a wall, turning its barrel at them. A rocket flashed through the air, and the tank exploded into flaming metal scraps. Murdock reloaded the launcher and waved for them to fall back.

His mike's interference screeched as Sanchez spoke. "I'm pulling back, there's too many of them. McCormick should be--" Hearing an explosion, Murdock looked up to see the bell tower collapse in a cascade of limestone.

"Sanchez, come in. McCormick, can you read me?"

"This is McCormick. I'm making my way to the fallback point. Sanchez is down. She stayed until the end so I could make it back."

Murdock winced and said, "Are there any more vehicles headed this way?"

"Two APCs surrounded by infantry are almost on top of your position. I can't engage them with my weapons."

"Noted. Get back ASAP and ready up for the final phase. Over and out." Spotting Vo, he dashed over and handed him the launcher. "Two APCs are coming. Wait until I give the signal to fire." Without waiting for an answer he rounded up the survivors of his group. Leading them up onto the roof, he pointed at a set of mortars. "Fire on my signal too."

Pulling out a rangefinder, he peered at the sky. A pair of light grey arrowheads shot through the clouds, consolidating into the VTOLs. "What the? They're too early..." A hand pulled him down as bullets parted the air above him. Peering over the edge, he saw the APCs rumble into view, machine gun bullets dimpling their armor plating. Despite the continuous fire, insurrectionist infantry crouched behind them, braving snapshots at the machine gun posts.

Murdock keyed his mike. "This is Sergeant Murdock to evac; there is hostile anti-air weaponry in the town." Harsh crackling static answered him in kind. "I repeat, there is hostile anti-air--"

The VTOLs approached the town and veered away from the square when they saw the APCs. They were too late, and in a hail of flak cannon shells one burst into flames, careening into the ground. As it broke apart, one of its engines slammed into an APC and exploded, engulfing its occupants in flames. The other transport flashed overhead, vanishing from view as it landed in the evac point.

"Fire!" In a series of thumps, airburst shells rained on the square, decimating the infantry foolish enough to follow the APCs. A rocket flashed out from the ground floor and struck the second APC in the side. Acrid black smoke billowed from the gaping hole, but its turret was still operational. Its flak cannon arced across the buildings, the explosive rounds tearing apart floors and decimating anyone caught in the blasts.

"Everyone fall back to the bridge!" Murdock and his men rappelled down the back and retreated towards the edge of the town, where a makeshift Alamo awaited them. Five other survivors including Vo and Dubbo were arming the

215

defenses for a final stand. McCormick stepped out from behind the bridge's gatehouse and waved at Murdock.

"I managed to contact the evac transport. They've secured the wounded and the package, but there's a problem." He eyed the distant flames and columns of smoke. "There's not enough space for even half of us if we make it. Most of us will have to stay behind."

Murdock cursed and looked at the remaining soldiers. "The jeep is still here, it can ferry people to the VTOL." He looked back at the corporal with a gaunt face. "But we still can't save everyone." Seeing him nod, Murdock placed a hand on his shoulder. "I need you to go, command will need a survivor to debrief. Take the critically wounded, and Dubbo too. That kid deserves better than a death sentence."

McCormick shook his head, his helmet straps swaying wildly. "But--"

"There's no time. This is an order soldier." The first wave of insurrectionists emerged from the rubble, and a machine gun thumped. McCormick sighed and fell back, leading three bloodied men to the jeep. Murdock crouched behind a pile of rubble and opened fire on the enemy, his rifle glowing red from the stream of bullets. Pausing to reload, he turned around to see Dubbo beside him.

"What the hell are you doing private?"

"I can't leave you to die, sir." He raised his carbine and sprayed a burst. "You deserve a chance." A hail of bullets chipped at the crude fort, and a paratrooper fell into the water with a grunt. Murdock pulled Dubbo down and stared at him.

"As do you. I've lived my life. You go live yours." He shook Dubbo. "Do you understand me soldier?" Grenades exploded several meters from them, caking everyone in granite dust. Murdock could hear Vo shout something about a troop transport.

Dubbo glanced around desperately, his eyes glistening. Turning back to Murdock, he sniffed and nodded. "Sir, yes, Sir!" He made a dash to where McCormick was hiding the jeep while everyone else moved to cover his escape.

Murdock slid over to the machine gun and pushed aside the dead ranger slumped against it. Taking one last look at Dubbo, he keyed his mike. "Listen to some Gorillaz for me, will ya?" The private glanced at him from the jeep's backseat, making a salute before vanishing in a cloud of dust.

Murdock turned back to the battle and racked the gun's charging handle. "Alright, let's show them how it's done, give it all you got." The defenders hunkered down for their last stand, launching waves of lead downrange at the enemy. His shoulders ached from the incessant kicking of the machine gun, but the insurrectionists kept filing through the kill zone. Bullets pinged off titanium as the troop transport barged through the piles of rubble. Its hexagonal gunner turret swiveled and roared, the shots tearing up chunks of the bridge as it tried to flush them out.

Grenades sent shrapnel tearing into the infantry that poured out from the back, but the transport kept advancing, its shots getting more accurate. Murdock was reloading the machine gun when an invisible hand threw him upwards. When he shook the stars from his eyes, he could see flames rising from the machine gun nest: a shell had flown into the remaining ammunition, resulting in an explosion.

Struggling to get up, he heard the sound of boots clattering against the stone. Pulling out his sidearm, Murdock was about to stand when a shadow flashed above him.

"Stay down Sarge, I've got this." A hand shoved him into the floor, and Vo vaulted across the rubble walls, firing his submachine gun from the hip. Reaching the middle of the bridge, he crouched behind a pile of bricks. "Bring up the last rocket!" The last two paratroopers rose and made a dash for the lance corporal.

One dived into a squad of enemy shock troopers, dumping her last magazine into them before spiraling into the river from a shotgun blast. The other strafed across the bridge, tossing the launcher just before the transport's turret reduced him to a scorch mark. It clattered across the stones, stopping just out of Vo's reach.

Murdock saw him glance between the launcher and the transport. "Don't do it, the blast will kill you."

Vo turned around and smiled at him. Before Murdock could rise, he rolled into the open and scooped up the weapon. A cloud of crimson appeared as a bullet ripped through his gut, but it was too late. As Vo collapsed he pulled the trigger, and a moment later a ten meter circle of blackened stone and scorched vehicle parts was the only evidence of his existence.

Murdock winced and huddled against the rubble. Looking down the road, he saw a light gray speck rise in the azure sky and veer to the west. His cracked eyepiece delivered one more message before fizzling out: **Package secured, returning to HQ. Thank you.** Wiping a tear from his eye, he smiled.

"You're welcome."

He pulled out a detonator for the demolition charges planted underneath the bridge, waiting for the infantry to get nearer. As the first head peered over the wall, he flipped the switch, and a blinding white light engulfed him.

Dubbo glanced out of the window at the blossoming red cloud. Wiping away the tears welling in his eyes, he laid back in his seat. He pulled out his battered media player, turning it around in his hand.

"Godspeed Sarge. I'll see you again someday."

# THE SOUND OF SILENCE
## By Monica Van

The sound of silence
Is an eerie hand against my ear,
The absence of interaction,
The black hole of communication.

At times, it may
Lack compassion.
It may be a weapon
Or a defense reaction
To injustice, indignation, ignorance,
Or rejection of opinion.

I hear the void
More often than not,
But I do not avoid it.
For at times,
It is compassion,
An understanding reaction,
The only way to say
What words can't.

The sound of silence
In the presence
Of a smile or a nod,
Or a pat or a hug
Of reassurance
Is not so much an eerie hand by the ear
As an acknowledgement
Of people near,
The reminder that
People are here, listening.

The sound of silence,
Rather than an eerie hand,
Is a lending hand
From a misunderstood ghost by the ear,
Reminding us that silence
Is nothing
To fear.

# AUTHOR BIOS

## DANIEL BUI

Born in Southern California, Daniel Bui has varied interests. He enjoys arts and crafts, as well as sports such as volleyball. He listens to classical music but also loves hip hop. Currently, his focus is on writing stories and poetry about the wonders of love.

## DIANE BUI

Hailing from the city of Fountain Valley, Diane Bui discovered the power of writing at a young age. As she grew, so did her imagination and writing skills. Armed with ideas old and new, Diane strives to design a world where anything can happen. In a book, of course.

## JENNIFER CHAU

Born in SoCal, Princess Jenn grew up with an obsession for flats shoes and writing. When she is not scribbling down ideas for a poem, play, or story with a cute font or a hot pink pen, Jennifer does DIY projects, dreams about travelling, or volunteers in her community.

## ANGELA CHHUN

Angela hopes to be an animator in the future. She joined the creative writing class to find creative inspiration. Being surrounded by so many writers with a sense a humor and imagination has taught her how to focus on creating a strong story-line in addition to her animations.

## EMILY DANG

Emily Dang is a young Asian-American aspiring to be known. Throughout her fourteen crazy years, Emily has acquired many skills: dance, music, and writing. As she continues on her journey of self-discovery, Emily hopes to inspire fellow peers through art.

## HUAN DAO

Born in Vietnam, Huan moved to the U.S at age nine which is when he discovered his love for scary movies and fiction. He is adventurous and unafraid to try new things. In the future, he plans to move to Los Angeles to pursue his passion of developing apps.

### KRISTY DIEP

Made with love from Southern California, Kristy has always lived in the Orange County area wishing to travel around the world and not only write of her journey but photograph it as well. She aspires to make a difference and change the faith of humanity through her inspiring words, hoping to one day achieve world peace.

### LILY DO

Lily Do is a mixture of dyed hair, yellow clothing, and a dash of La Quinta pride. She aspires to lead others to greatness and increase school spirit. If needed to be found, she is stuffed in her locker, lying on the ground, or banging her head to EDM.

### TUYET DUONG

Spawned in beautiful SoCal, Tuyet "Mother Twiggered" Duong grew up loving writing and food. Although small in stature, Twiggy harbors immeasurable rage whenever someone calls her short.

### LEIANNA GIRYAN

Born and raised in southern California, Leianna Giryan has always enjoyed video games and anything within the sci-fi genre. She is terrible with enunciation and any form of speaking, but she voices herself through writing poetry and thrillers. Leianna aspires to help people in and out of the classroom.

### CHRISTINE HA

Christine Ha yearns for the arts, both visual and written. She is beginning her creative journey. With her imaginative brain packed with ideas, she creates original artwork and literature. Destiny has no part in her life--just diligence and experience.

### JOSEPH HO

Joseph Ho grew up in Orange County, Santa Ana and never left. He lived his childhood drawing sketches on the walls, paper, and in his sketchbook. He enjoyed drawing and painting so much, he expressed it in stories too. This is his first publication.

### CHEYENNE DANIELLE HUNT

Growing up in a small horse town in California, Cheyenne loves to drive cross country on long road trips with her friends. Wildly creative and strong-willed, she adores nature with a passion. She constantly seeks adventure. Music flows freely through her soul.

### VICENTE MARI INCIONG

Born in the Philippines, Vince Inciong lived there for fifteen years before moving to the USA where he explored hobbies that best expressed his creativity. He enjoys theater and writing, as well as playing video games. He feels writing allows him to immortalize special memories with loved ones.

### KENNA B. JAMES

Kenna B. James grew up in Orange County and had few friends but didn't mind because she was naturally creative and often in her own world. She loves reading books and writing stories, and since she discovered she had the talent, she loved writing even more.

### LINDA LAM

A person of few words, Linda often daydreams and finds it easier to write out her thoughts and feelings rather than speaking them. When she was younger, she lost herself in books and now that she is older, she is rediscovering herself by writing her own story.

### BRYAN LE

Bryan Le is someone who you simultaneously want to be around and don't. Puns are pillar in his life.

### BECKY LEE

Becky is a young meme who enjoys writing adventure stories and poetry. "Sleepless Nights" is her first published poem. Other than writing, she enjoys creating graphic designs and eating good food.

### KATIE LUONG

Katie Luong is an optimistic young lady. Originally born in San Bernardino, she decided to move down to Orange County. By day, she is a writer and by night a reader. In love with the world culture, she dreams of traveling the globe as a worldwide journalist.

### JAYSON MITCHELL

Originally from Nevada, Jayson Mitchell traveled extensively and experienced many cultures. Fascinated by stories, he began writing in second grade. Since then, he has refined his writing, hoping to become an author who inspires others to take arms with pen and paper.

### KATIA NAVARRETTE

Originally from California, Katia Navarrete grew up in the city of Garden Grove where she discovered her love of reading, writing and drawing. She began writing stories and poems in her early teen years in hopes to be published. Katia aspires to leave her mother´s home and become a teacher.

### ANGELINA NGO

Born in California but raised in Hawaii, Angelina grew up with a fierce passion for writing. She spent her childhood mesmerized by books, reading whenever she could. Although teased by many, Angelina remains optimistic and curious to find out what the world has in store for her.

### ANDREA NGUYEN

Andrea Nguyen grew up in Westminster California where she used her wild imagination to write stories. In second grade, she was given a "Best Author" award and hasn't let the title go; she still reminds everyone. However, as perfect as her life may seem, she is still working on herself to go down as the most amazing person alive.

## COLLEEN NGUYEN

Her journey begins in Fountain Valley, where Colleen Nguyen does little things like daydream and search for adventure, finding inspiration to write. With a notebook full of ideas and a pencil in hand, Colleen allows her mind to wander while the world around her continues moving.

## DEREK NGUYEN

Born in Thousand Oaks, Derek Nguyen spent the majority of his life in Westminster where he discovered Star Wars, 70's rock, 80's pop, and Legos. His "Freedom for a Day" that appears in this anthology is his first published work. He hopes to one day achieve his dream of becoming a medical researcher.

## HELEN NGUYEN

Helen Nguyen grew up in California, and although scared of the unfathomable ocean depths, she appreciates the sound of waves and sea scent. She loves cacti, cats, coffee, and collecting journals. This year she plans to fill in those pages with doodles, adventures, and daydreams. Helen aspires to be a cat lady with a small studio apartment and window sill for her plants.

## JENNY NGUYEN

Jenny Nguyen is a 17 year-old dreamer who adores her pet dog, Russell. Her hobbies include writing fantasy stories, reading adventure novels, composing music, playing video games, and drawing portraits. She hopes to one day publish her own book and become an English teacher.

## KIMBERLY NGUYEN

Growing up in Southern California, Kimberly Nguyen has had a fascination with her books of childhood fairy tales. She began story writing for her family which has since morphed into a love for writing and poetry. Seeking a future career working with animals, Kimberly's passion for nature is reflected through her work.

## KRISTY NGUYEN

Kristy Nguyen grew up in Fountain Valley surrounded by Asian cuisine and boba. Being a bit forgetful and klutzy at times doesn't stop her from working towards her dreams. Kristy aspires to be a short story author and poet in the future.

## VINCENT NGUYEN

After moving to Fountain Valley from Westminster, Vincent spent much of his time nurturing his love for fiction through reading, drawing, gaming, and (of course) writing. Though his ideal dream is to make choose-your-own-adventure novels, he has settled with attempting to write shorter prose for experience.

## ANGEL NUNEZ

Angel Nunez was born in November in Anaheim. He moved from apartment to apartment before settling down in a mobile home in Garden Grove, his childhood home, and more recently, Santa Ana. He is currently a senior at La Quinta High School where he is exploring his interests in screenwriting.

## THONG PHAM

Thong Thien Pham—eccentric, visionary, rebel—spent his childhood and adolescence in Southern California. In his early days, he was quite adamant against writing, but great books and greater teachers awoke his love for it. He aspires to be successful in law, like love.

## ALEXANDRA QUANG

A student in the city Westminster, Alexandra Quang is a girl who indulges her ideas in the forms of writing and recording her work on anything but paper.

## MIKAYLA REILLY

Growing up in Westminster, California, Mikayla Reilly thrived to find her purpose in life. Upon entering high school, she had loyal and caring friends who introduced her to the art of the fangirl. From that point on, Mikayla knew she only needed to do one thing: fangirl.

## GABRIELLE ROMERO

Gabbi Romero is from Garden Grove where she enjoys movies, long walks on the beach, and head-banging to loud rock music. She's a dedicated, outgoing individual who takes no prisoners. Her signature pose is the reverse over-the-shoulder-triple-axle akimbo. Most importantly, she loves her family and dedicates everything she does to them with love and gratitude.

## CHLOE SHANE SANCHEZ

Born in Philippines, Chloe Sanchez traveled to United States where she discovered many interests. She likes writing, drawing, sleeping and watching her regular shows. Her favorite things: chocolate, spaghetti, dogs and vacations. Chloe's goal is to become a dentist and make her parents proud.

## TYLER TA

Born in Illinois, Tyler Ta grew up in California gaining an interest in video games, golfing, and drawing. "World of Mine craft" is his first published poem. Although not entirely certain, Tyler currently wants to work somewhere in the agricultural fields.

## APRIL THONG

Determined to make her own webtoons and perhaps, mangas, April enrolled in a creative writing course as well as a computer graphics class during her senior year in high school. This is a result of her works.

## MAGGIE TIEU

Maggie Tieu aspires to become a fictional story writer or an animator on a children's cartoon show. Outside her bustling senior life in high school with nothing but tear-jerking deadlines, Maggie often watches one of her all-time favorite cartoons, "Gravity Falls," created by Alex Hirsch.

## VYLAN TRAN

Vylan was born and raised in Fountain Valley, California, the state where magic is made. She loves drawing, singing, playing the piano, and the color yellow. Manga, anime and especially games inspired her to write her own romantic stories. "SHE" is her first publication. In the future, she hopes to create her own Anime series.

## MONICA VAN

Native to California, Monica Van grew up in Santa Ana where she discovered her creativity. Her first published works appeared in *When You Give a Creative Writing Class a Deadline* and *Pages of the Mind*, and she will continue to hone her writing skills even after high school graduation.

## PETER VU

Peter Vu was born and raised in Orange County, California where he discovered his love for oceans and writing. This is Peter's first publication. He hopes one day to write screenplays.

## AAMIR YUSUF

Aamir Yusuf is a tall fellow with aspiration to be a Filmmaker and Actor. He's performed in many school plays and one of his favorite directors is Quentin Tarantino.

www.ingramcontent.com/pod-product-compliance
Lightning Source LLC
Chambersburg PA
CBHW060323260626
47160CB00007B/2662